COACHING HIS BABYGIRL

RORY REYNOLDS

to all the wallflowers waiting to bloom

Who knew a flat tire could change your life?

Only I would manage to stumble upon a private club like The Playground. I'm a curvy little band teacher, innocent to what goes on in a club like this.

But I want to learn...everything. My curiosity is piqued, and I can't turn away.

And then I see him. The man I've been obsessed with for the last three years.

Cooper Crane.

He thinks I'm innocent.
 Vanilla.
 That I don't crave what he can give me... that I don't melt when he makes me call him daddy.

He's everything I shouldn't want, and everything I need.

———

Sign up for Rory Reynolds newsletter and never miss a release. Sign up here or go to www.roryreynoldsromance.com

CHAPTER ONE

Melinda

I TAKE A STEADYING breath and wipe my palms on my skirt, trying to settle my nerves before opening the door to the restaurant where Darlene's birthday party is being held. One look at how nice the restaurant is inside, and I feel out of place in my casual long skirt and pink button-up shirt.

After a quick look, I see Cooper standing just off to one side of the hostess station talking to a gorgeous redhead. I slowly, nervously, make my way to where he's standing. He turns toward me and smiles, making his dark eyes shine. I feel my cheeks heat with a blush at his attention.

"Mel," he growls in that low tenor of his.

"Hi Coop," I say to the tips of my shoes. Ugh. I hate how shy I get around him... well, not just him, but it's especially bad around Cooper Crane. He's the most handsome man I've ever seen in my life.

He's tall, built, and has a strong jaw that could cut stone that even his beard can't hide. He's also fifteen years my senior and doesn't know I exist beyond being coworkers at Thurston Academy.

"Mel, this is Tessa, Jasper, and Ransom."

I raise my fingers and give them a little wiggle of hello. My nerves are on overdrive at being introduced to strangers. Tessa gives me a bright smile and moves to my side.

"You must be the brilliant band teacher that Darlene can't stop talking about. She recommended a couple of books you've gotten her to read..." Tessa waggles her eyebrows. "Definite page-turners."

I feel the heat of my cheeks as they turn bright red from embarrassment. I know exactly what books she's talking about. Naughty romance... my dirty little secret. I might be a buttoned-up virgin, but I love my romance books. It all started with my grandmother's bodice rippers when I was way too young to be reading them. Now my tastes run a little darker... kinkier.

Tessa must sense my discomfort because she quickly changes the subject to Darlene's birthday and how excited she is. I only half pay attention because one of the other patrons grabs my attention. A woman dressed in head-to-toe leather walks up to Coop and kisses both his cheeks in greeting. Jealousy flashes through me even though I have no claim to him. He must feel my eyes on him because he turns towards me. I quickly avert my gaze and it's then I notice the attire of some of the other patrons.

Leather, corsets, schoolgirl uniforms on women much too old to be schoolgirls, and more. My eyes are bouncing from person to person so I don't notice how close Coop has gotten until he lifts me out of the way of a man who stumbles directly into the path of where I was just standing.

Coop growls low in his throat and tells the man to watch where he's going. The man holds his hands up and apologizes. The possessive way his hand rests at my lower back and the low growl of his warning to the stranger has butterflies taking flight in my stomach. My nerves are dancing on a tightwire at his closeness. I've had a huge crush on Coop since the day I started working at Thurston Academy three years ago.

What red-blooded woman wouldn't have a crush? He's what one would call a silver fox. He's built like the ex-football player he is, with broad shoulders and thick muscles all over. He practically towers over me at six foot three. The first day I saw him out on the football field working out with the team... shirtless... I nearly swallowed my tongue. I did trip over my own feet and barely caught myself from faceplanting.

The sweat glistening on his chest, the way the sun shone down on his salt and pepper hair... the gruff way he counted down whatever exercise he had his team running. All of it is burned into my memory. Coop's hand lightly moves over my lower back, and I shiver. Did I say butterflies? More like a gaggle of geese.

I'm slowly burning up inside and no one seems to notice. Surely someone can see the steam coming off of me. But no, I'm standing here simmering and no one is the wiser. Just as I'm about to spontaneously combust from Coop's touch, the doors open admitting Darlene and Colt.

Darlene's eyes light up when she sees us standing here. She wraps first Tessa, then me up in a big hug. "Thank you so much for coming!"

I smile, happy that my friend is happy that I came. I might be in the deep end as far as my comfort zone goes, but knowing that Darlene's birthday is just a little more special because I bravely stepped out of the comfort zone that I stay firmly planted in makes me feel good.

"Our table is ready," Tessa says happily. "We were just waiting for you to get here." Tessa gives a knowing wink and giggles.

A gorgeous woman wearing a black mini skirt and mesh shirt over a silver bra leads us to an empty table in the middle of the room. My mind can't even think about how odd her attire is with Cooper's hand on my lower back, guiding me through the restaurant. When he pulls out my chair, I swoon.

I've never had someone do that for me; it's right out of one of my romance novels.

I close my eyes, taking a deep breath and doing my best to center myself before I float away on my fantasies of Coop doing these things because he's even half as attracted to me as I am to him.

Ridiculous.

He'd never choose a woman as shy as I am. He belongs with someone like Tessa, bold and beautiful. Proud of her curves and willing to show them off instead of hiding behind her loose skirts and tops. I'm the exact opposite of the kind of woman a man like Coop should be with.

Dinner seems to go by quickly. I think the food is good, but I honestly can't remember tasting a single bite, not with the heat of Coop sitting right beside me. Not when his rumbly voice dances over my skin as he chats with his friends.

Once everyone is done eating and the dinner party is winding down, I get up to excuse myself. Darlene stands and gives me a tight hug, thanking me for coming.

"Thanks for having me," I say shyly.

Coop stands from the table. "I'll walk you out." He states it as fact, leaving zero room for argument. He gives Darlene a friendly hug, wishing her happy birthday, then his hand is on my lower back again. Goosebumps cover my skin, and my nipples harden inside my bra. I feel like a total pervert at being turned on from such a simple, platonic touch. My body has gone completely rogue.

We get outside in the cool night air and I take a deep, steadying breath. I do my best to draw my attention away from his hand on my back.

"You don't have to walk me to my car," I say, finally finding my voice.

Coop gives me a look of annoyance but says nothing.

"Alrighty then," I say more to myself than anything.

We get to my car and he takes my keys from my hand and unlocks the door and opens it for me. Another gentlemanly thing that I've never had happen to me before. Swoon. So much swoon.

"Thanks," I whisper.

"You're welcome." His gruff tone sends another shiver down my spine. Lord, this man is too sexy for his own good.

I climb into the car and reach to close the door, but Coop holds fast to the door. "Buckle up," he growls.

I give him a sideways look but do as he instructs. The moment the belt clicks in place, he releases his hold on the door. Before I can reach for it, he closes me into the car. I can't help but smile at the small ways he just took care of me. It reminds me of some of my favorite naughty books. The only thing that would've made it better is a 'good girl' or two thrown in for my good behavior.

Goodness, I'm a mess. Like Cooper would ever in a million years say something like that. I wouldn't even know what to do with myself. I'm a virgin for crying out loud. What man in their right mind would want to take on a virgin who has dreams of being called a good girl and taken over her daddy's knee?

I start my car and pull out of my parking spot. I drive away, watching Coop get smaller and smaller in my rearview. Such a strange night. That has to be why my mind is playing tricks on me. Seeing things that aren't there. He was just being kind, not showing any kind of desire for me, and yet I was ready to melt at his feet like a puddle of hussy.

I'm two blocks away when I hear a low pop, and the wheel jerks in my hand. I quickly pull over to the side of the road and put a hand over my heart which is beating out of my chest. After a deep, steadying breath, I get out of the car and walk to the passenger side, immediately seeing the flat tire.

"Damn it," I grumble.

I get back in my car and start searching through my purse for my phone but come up empty.

"Double damn."

I rarely use my cell phone. It's for emergencies. I don't have many friends, and I'm not into social media so there's not much need to be tied to the device like other people my age. Of course, now that I have an emergency and my phone is nowhere to be found, I almost wish I was tied to my phone like other people are.

I rest my head on the steering wheel and bang it lightly. The only thing I can do is walk back to the restaurant and ask to use their phone. There aren't any other businesses in this area. This is mostly an industrial part of town, so even if the businesses were open, they're not the kind of place you just wander into.

The street is dark, and the abandoned feel of the area has chills running up and down my spine. I grab my purse, lock up the car and head back the way I came on foot. I'm near the restaurant when I see a building with a small sign that says, "The Playground." The lights are on, and it's bright inside. Maybe it's some kind of indoor play yard for kids; why else would a business be called The Playground?

I feel safe going inside and asking to use their phone. Plus, it cuts down on a whole lot of walking outside in the dark. Win-win.

I open the door and am greeted by a smiling receptionist. I instantly recognize her from the restaurant as one of the patrons... it's then I notice the same corset and booty shorts she was wearing to dinner. Definitely not the kind of outfit you'd wear working for a children's play yard.

"Hello. Are you here to meet someone?" she asks with a smile. Her eyes widen in what looks like recognition. "Oh, you're here for Coach Cooper, aren't you?"

I must look confused because she turns her head to one side. "You were at dinner with Coach, right?"

I nod slowly. Wondering to myself why she's calling Coop Coach? And why is that my concern at the moment and not the fact that she's dressed so provocatively at a play place for children?

"I just need to see your ID, then you can enter the club."

Club? I should just ask to use the phone and go, but I'm curious as to what is happening behind that darkened door and what Coop has to do with it. That's the only reason I can explain why I hand my driver's license over without any questions. The woman pulls out a piece of paper and pushes it in my direction. "Just a standard nondisclosure."

That should concern me, but instead, it further piques my curiosity. I sign the paper quickly, and the woman smiles wider. "You're free to go inside. Have fun playing," she says perkily.

Is this an adult playground, then? So many questions but only one way to answer them. I open the door and stumble inside. I curse my clumsiness, ready to be embarrassed and have a roomful of people staring at me, but no one is paying attention.

It takes me a moment to get my bearings as I

take in the large room. The centerpiece of the room is a large playground like what you would see in any park in the city. Only the equipment is adult-sized. A smile spreads across my face at the thought of a place where adults can come and play. I wander further into the room and see a lovely sitting area to my left with several men and women chatting and laughing.

I do a double-take when I see a woman in nothing but her bra and panties chatting with a man wearing overalls looking much more like a boy than a man. I try hard not to judge. To each their own and all that, but this place is... odd.

I walk past the sitting area and see a bar that looks like one from any club. Well, at least the ones I've seen on TV and read about in books.

"Hey, girl!" Tessa says, scaring the crap out of me. She's out of the pretty dress she wore to dinner and is wearing a naughty schoolgirl outfit. I give her a confused look but don't get a chance to say anything before she's threading her arm through mine and guiding me toward the bar. "What are you doing here?" she asks her voice tight.

"F-flat tire. Forgot my phone."

"That sucks. I think Coop is at the bar with Ransom..." she says with a roll of her eyes.

"Oh..."

"You are here for him, right?"

My attention is drawn away from Tessa when a

topless woman walks by being led on a leash. It is not the kind of leash that would be hooked to a collar, but one of those worn around the chest with a stuffie on it... like what you use for a young child. The man leading her is wearing a tailored suit and looks stern. I watch with curious eyes, rubbernecking to keep watching as Tessa leads me away, pulling me steadily to the bar.

"What is this place?" I ask as more of the room comes into view. To the right of the bar is a huge area with tons of toys and grown men and women playing animatedly. My stomach clenches, and I feel a pang of jealousy at their freedom. How long has it been since I've felt that level of carefreeness?

"Um..." Tessa starts giving me a worried look, "maybe Coop should explain."

I look back at Tessa as she drags me back to the bar. She doesn't look around; instead, she leads me directly to one end, where I immediately see Cooper and Ransom. Coop raises a glass with amber liquid to his lips and drinks deeply.

Ransom sees me first, and his eyes widen. He taps Coop's arm and nods toward me. Coop turns, and his jaw drops looking gobsmacked when he sees me walking towards him. I would giggle if I didn't feel the enormity of this situation. I feel like something significant is about to happen. I just have no idea what it could be.

CHAPTER TWO

Cooper

THE LAST PERSON I expected to see in the club tonight is Melinda Young. What on earth is my sweet band teacher doing here? How did she even get inside? Only members and their guests are allowed inside.

Tessa leads her towards me with wide, almost panicked eyes. I try to stay calm, but this is not how I envisioned introducing her to The Playground. And trust me, I have imagined it often. I've kept my desires hidden because Mel is as vanilla as they come. Shy, sweet, beautiful... she's everything I've ever wanted, but so far out of my reach it's almost painful.

"Mel, is something wrong?" I ask, trying to draw her attention to me instead of the rest of the club. She's not focused on me at all. Her eyes wander around the room with what looks like wide-eyed wonder. I put a knuckle under her chin and lightly guide her eyes to mine. "Mel?"

"Flat tire," she mumbles, her eyes wandering again.

"Eyes on me, kitten."

That gets her attention. I didn't mean to say it, but her being here and curious as a kitten, the endearment just rolled off my tongue. It feels damn good too.

"You got a flat? Why didn't you call someone?"

"I forgot my phone," she says, flushing with embarrassment. "I thought this was a... playground for children."

Her head turns to the large playground equipment where littles are playing happily. I try to see it through vanilla eyes and can only imagine what she's thinking.

"What is this place?" she asks, sounding more than curious... maybe a little in awe.

Tessa looks between the two of us and winces. She knows Mel is as vanilla as they come and obviously doesn't envy me the upcoming conversation.

Ransom comes up and grabs Tessa by the arm. "Let's give them some privacy, brat."

Usually, Tessa would protest Ransom's heavy-handedness, but this time she quickly makes her escape. Traitor.

With a hand on Mel's lower back, I lead her to a quiet corner, keeping her in the bar area, the most vanilla part of the club. Mel walks with her head turned, doing her best to see everything she can. She nearly bumps into someone, and I tuck her into my side. I'm thankful that the club is fairly quiet tonight because there's an open barstool at the end of the bar.

I lift her onto the stool and stand in front of her, blocking her view of the rest of the club. She looks up at me with big blue-gray eyes.

"What is this place?" she asks again.

"This is an exclusive club."

"What kind?"

Of course, a vague answer would never satisfy her curiosity, but it was worth a try. I rub my hand on the back of my neck, unsure exactly how much to tell her. What will satisfy her curiosity without shocking her?

"Have you heard of BDSM?" I ask, starting at the most basic of questions.

Her cheeks heat with a pretty pink blush, and her eyes move from mine down to my chest.

"Have you?" I repeat.

Mel nods shyly. "I've read books..."

"Well, this is a specialty club for a specific subset of the BDSM lifestyle."

She blinks up at me and shifts on her seat, trying to look past me every bit the curious kitten.

"What kind?" she asks, licking her berry pink lips.

"The Playground is for daddy doms and littles."

She licks her lips again, interest flaring in her eyes. Surely that isn't interest... I have to be imagining it—wishful thinking, perhaps.

"Do you know what that means?"

"Yes..." she nods and tries to look past me again.

I grip her chin more firmly than before. "Eyes on me, curious kitten."

"Sorry," she murmurs.

"Don't apologize for your curiosity, but I need to make sure you understand what you're seeing."

Her eyes widen, and she looks at me like a lightbulb just went off in her mind. "Are you a dominant or a submissive?"

I laugh a full belly laugh, and Mel pouts up at me prettily. I want to kiss that pout from her lips.

"I'm all dominant, babygirl."

"Oh," she says, breathless, her eyes dilated with what looks like desire. "You're a daddy?"

My cock is instantly hard behind my zipper at that word falling from her sweet lips. I want to kiss off the taste of every syllable.

"Yes," I growl, stepping between her legs. She gasps at my nearness and licks her lips. Her eyes are wide and her breaths shallow, but she doesn't say anything.

"What are you thinking, kitten?"

Her cheeks heat with a blush again, and I have a feeling that I know exactly what's on her mind and it's the same thing that's on mine. My thoughts are confirmed when she licks her lips and looks from my eyes to my lips. She wants me to kiss her. The temptation is great, but somehow I manage to withstand it.

"I like you calling me that." She gasps and covers her mouth like she's shocked the words came out of her lips.

I chuckle at her honesty and adorableness. "I like calling you that, sweet Mel."

She's quiet for a minute. I want nothing more than to show her everything the club can offer her but know it's too soon and may never happen despite my desires. Just because the curvy band teacher has had my cock rock-hard for the last three years doesn't mean anything.

She's vanilla and as innocent as the day she was born. She deserves better than a jaded man fifteen years her senior. Though the way she's looking at me right now makes me wonder if she could want me as badly as I want her. I shake my head, washing that thought from my mind.

"Let's go get your car fixed up."

She nods, licking those plump lips of hers again, her eyes still on mine.

I lift her carefully from the stool and guide her

away from the bar and toward the lobby and exit. Mel takes in everything she can as we walk. Her lips turn down in a pout when we are finally outside. She definitely wants to spend more time in the club. A little part of me is hopeful that she would like to explore things.

"Where'd you break down?"

She points to the left. "A couple blocks that way."

"You walked in this neighborhood in the dark? Alone?" I growl. "I should put you over my knee."

She gasps in outrage... or maybe it's longing because she looks far from upset about my threat.

"Or maybe my innocent kitten would like her punishment," I murmur teasingly in her ear.

She lets out a shuddering sigh, and I start questioning how vanilla she really is. Maybe Mel has secrets too.

"No more walking alone at night, young lady."

"I-I forgot my phone. What was I supposed to do?" she asks, sounding contrite.

I grow lowly. "No more forgetting your phone either."

She nods her head but looks down at her toes looking every bit the chastised little girl. My cock responds instantly to her demure behavior. I lead her to my truck and help her inside. I reach across her, the back of my hand lightly rubbing across her breasts as I stretch the belt over her lap. She shivers, her nipples pebbling beneath the thin material of her shirt.

I can't hold back my low groan. If she were mine, I would tease those nipples into hard peaks until she's whimpering for more. But... she's not mine. Not yet.

"I can do that," she complains as I click the belt into place.

"So can I," I say softly, letting her know I want to take care of her in this way.

Mel's lips tip up in a shy smile. "Thank you," she whispers.

I shut her safely in the truck and walk around to the driver's side. She's quiet as we drive towards her car. It's not an uncomfortable silence. I can tell she's just trying to absorb what she's seen tonight. I want to ask her what's on her mind but now isn't the time or place. She needs time to absorb everything before I start probing for her thoughts.

We get to her car, and I pull in behind it. Her rear passenger tire is flat just like she said. "Stay here, and I'll get you fixed up."

She hands me the keys to her car, and even though I can see the protest hanging on her lips, she doesn't vocalize it. I have to bite back the 'good girl' that I instinctually want to call her. That part of me deep inside who hopes beyond hope that she was intrigued by the club and wants to know more. Lord knows I want to show her everything.

I make quick work of getting her tire replaced with her spare. "All fixed. You'll need to get a new tire so you aren't without a spare," I tell her after I open the truck door.

"I will. Thanks for helping me," she says shyly. She unbuckles her seatbelt, and I help her down from the truck and guide her to her car, opening the door for her.

"No need to thank me." Her cheeks flush pink, and it's the most alluring thing I've ever seen. Unable to help myself, I lightly brush my fingertips over her pink cheek. "It was my pleasure, kitten."

Mel's lips tip up in a small smile before she climbs into the car. "Buckle up." She does what I say immediately, like the good girl she is. "I'm going to follow you home to make sure you get there safely."

"Oh, you don't have to do that, Coop."

"I do. If something happens, you don't have a phone to call for help."

She chews her lower lip then nods. "Thank you."

"What did I say about thanking me?"

"That I don't have to."

"That's right. It's always going to be my pleasure to do things for you."

I close her in the car, hating that our time together is over. She starts her car, waiting until I start my truck to pull away—such a good girl. Mel drives carefully home and pulls into the driveway of a cute little bungalow-style house that suits her perfectly. I park on the curb and watch her until she's safely inside her house. She gives me a little wave before closing the door.

CHAPTER THREE

Melinda

I WATCH Coop drive away from the window. I can't help questioning if tonight really happened. Did I really stumble into a sex club? A real for real BDSM club that not only is my closest friend Darlene a part of but the man I've been crushing on for years now.

Crazy.

Sleep doesn't come easy for me. I can't quit thinking about what I saw at The Playground. Once I do finally doze off, my dreams are plagued with Cooper and The Playground. My subconscious runs wild with possibilities. So much so that I wake up wet and needy. So needy that I slip my fingers under the waistband of my panties and touch my wetness.

I'm not unfamiliar with masturbation. I might be a twenty-seven-year-old virgin, but I've gotten myself off plenty of times... I've just never felt this kind of desire before. My pussy is hot and soaked, my clit overly sensitive. My fingers slip through my slickness, teasing up and around my clit, causing me to gasp at the light touch. I circle my clit imagining what it would feel like to have Cooper's fingers on me instead of my own. How rough his calloused hands would feel. Would he go soft and slow, or would he drive me over the edge in a fervor of passion?

Then my mind goes to even naughtier thoughts. Coop tipping me over his lap and spanking me with his big palm. Part of me wishes I knew what it felt like to be spanked, but another part is scared of how badly it might hurt. That thought pushes me closer to climax. I dip my fingers into my pussy and thrust them in and out, my thumb pressing against my clit. I throw my head back against my pillow, moaning into the empty room as my orgasm flows through my body.

I don't stop fucking myself with my fingers until I've eked out every ounce of pleasure. I collapse back to the bed breathless. A naughty thought of Cooper bringing his wet fingers to my lips and making me suck them clean comes to mind. I'm tempted to clean mine, pretending that he's ordering me to do it, but I restrain myself.

I get up and quickly clean up before I can give in to such a dirty temptation. I'm definitely not acting like myself. I've also never come so hard in my entire life. If just thinking about Coop is enough to get me off so powerfully, how would the real thing be? I shiver at the thought, reminding myself that there's no way that will ever happen. I'm not Cooper's type at all. He's the kind of man who would be with the sexy cheerleader, not the geeky band nerd.

I let out a rough sigh. Don't get me wrong, I love who I am. I love making music, but sometimes I wish I could be that sexy siren. Before I can fall down that rabbit hole of self-doubt my phone rings. I barely make it to it before it rings off to voicemail. I answer with a breathless hello.

"Hey, girl!" Darlene says cheerfully.

"Uh, hi," I stumble on my words. I don't talk on the phone often, and Darlene has never once called me, so it feels weird. "Is everything okay?"

"Oh, yes," she giggles. "Everything is great. I just wanted to check on you. I heard from Tessa last night."

Ah. It makes sense now. She's calling to check up on me from my little impromptu visit to The Playground. "I'm okay. Why wouldn't I be?"

This time Darlene's giggle is a little strained. "Well, I mean... you did just find out that there is a sex club, and several of your friends are members."

"Well..." I don't really know what to say. I haven't really given much thought to the fact that her and Colt are part of the same club as Coop. Maybe that should bother me more than it does. I mean, my closest friend has kept a huge secret from me. I decide to go with honesty, "I don't know how I should feel right now."

"Fair enough. So did Cooper give you a tour of the place?" Darlene sounds way more excited about the prospect than she should. If I didn't know better, I would say she set it up. But she couldn't have because a flat tire and maybe fate brought me to The Playground's doorstep.

"No... he escorted me out pretty quickly. Though we did talk a little about what the club is and that he's a daddy dom." I slap my forehead. "I asked if he was a submissive."

She giggles. "Cooper? A submissive?"

I plop down on my couch and cover my face with my hand. "I know, I'm such a dummy."

"Oh shush," she scolds. "You're not a dummy. I'm sure you were just shellshocked. I mean, it's not every day you find out your friends are kinky."

"This is true. It was like a page out of one of my books," I admit to seeing the parallel.

"Now you know why I like the books so much!" Darlene giggles.

"I never would have guessed. Though I can totally see Colt being dominant. He's got that air about him."

"He is totally dominant... So tell me... what did you think of the club?"

I chew on my bottom lip, unsure on how much I

want to reveal. I hardly know myself how I feel about it. I think part of me is still in shock, and then there's the whole masturbating to thoughts of Cooper spanking me thing.

"It was definitely interesting."

"Hmm. Interesting like you want to learn more or interesting like we're all crazy?" she asks.

"I honestly didn't realize there was such a place. Of course, I know about BDSM clubs, but a place that is special just for daddy doms and littles. I had no idea. I'll admit I'm curious. But just because I read about it doesn't necessarily mean I want it in real life."

I feel my cheeks flush because I can taste the lie on my tongue. I'm thankful that I'm on the phone because I'm a terrible liar. One look, and Darlene would call me out.

"But you do want it. Don't you?" she asks boldly.

My sigh comes straight from the tips of my toes. "I honestly don't know. It stirred something inside me..."

"So you and Colt are both members like Cooper?" I ask. Even though I know the answer, I'm just trying to change the subject and not very smoothly.

She giggles. "Yes. Of course. It's how I met Tessa and Ransom."

"Why didn't you ever tell me?" I ask, feeling a little hurt.

"I wasn't sure how you would respond. It's not something easily brought up in conversation."

"I can see that." I gnaw on my bottom lip, abusing it more today than I have ever in my life. It's a nervous tick. "And Coop is a daddy dom?" I ask even though he already told me he was. I want to hear more, and this is my horrible segue into the topic.

"Yes, he is."

"Does he have a little?" I ask, not sure at all if I want to know the answer. I hold my breath as I await Darlene's response.

"He's single. I think he's got his eye on someone though," she says almost teasingly.

Jealousy runs rampant through my entire being. I hate the thought of Coop with someone else. But he's a daddy dom, and I'm not a little. It couldn't possibly be me who he wants, though that's what Darlene implies. Unless I'm reading too much into her words.

"So, how do you feel about everything?"

How do I feel? Curious. Excited. Horny. Terrified. So many things that I can't land on just one. "Curious..."

Darlene laughs. "I can understand that one. There's a lot to be curious about."

"No kidding," I sigh and lay back on the couch.

"What about Coop?" she asks.

"What about him?"

"Are you curious about him?"

I blush and stutter. To admit the truth or not? Once again, I decide to go with the truth. "Very curious."

Darlene squeals in my ear. "I knew it! You two are perfect for each other."

"Uh... one little problem with that..."

She laughs again. "Don't think that's going to be a problem for long," she says confidently.

I can't help but to wonder what she's talking about. Is she insinuating that I'm a little? Is that possible? Or is she thinking that Cooper will change to be what I need? So many questions and not enough answers. I hate feeling so off-center and in the dark, especially when it's my own feelings causing the issue.

I hear Colt say something in the background, then breathless giggles from Darlene. "Gotta go," she says abruptly.

"Okay. Bye."

Well, that phone call answered some of my questions and gave me about a million more. I'm even more curious and confused than I was thirty minutes ago. I shake my head, dislodging the thoughts. Time to shower and get on with my Sunday.

The hot water feels heavenly. I take extra time shaving every inch of my skin and double condition my hair. After my shower, I slather lotion over my skin, pampering myself. I dress in a cute pair of leggings that hug my curves and a slouchy shirt that hangs off one shoulder. Basically the opposite of my regular day-to-day clothes. This is what I consider my Sunday best. Comfy clothes for doing chores and running errands.

I put on some music then start my laundry. After I've vacuumed and scrubbed my kitchen, I decide to go to the grocery store before I clean the bathroom. I swap out my laundry, then sit down with a bag of Cheetos (my guilty pleasure) and write out my shopping list.

My trip to the store is a quick one. It's a small benefit to living alone. I don't require much. I turn down my street and furrow my brow and the big black truck parked in front of my house. I recognize it as Coop's right away. A thrill of excitement followed by nervousness floods my system.

I pull into my driveway and turn off the engine. What on earth is he doing here? I quickly pull up my big girl panties and get out of the car. No use trying to hide because I get the feeling he's pretty persuasive and will easily talk me out of my car.

He climbs out of his truck and walks toward me. I do my best to keep from drooling at his tight jeans and white t-shirt. The sun shines around him, high-lighting the silver in his dark hair. It glints in the sunlight, making him look every bit the silver fox he is.

His smile is broad and welcoming with just a bit of sexy smolder. I nearly collapse into a puddle of embarrassed goo when he looks me up and down. It only takes me a minute to remember what I'm wearing today. It's the first time he's seen me out of my usual long skirts or dresses. I blush at the heated look he gives me.

I lick my lips, gathering my courage. "What are you doing here?" I ask.

"I wanted to check in on you after last night," he says with a warm smile

"Oh." I look down at the ground feeling extra shy. Did he talk to Darlene? Oh God, what would she have told him? No, I shake away that thought. She wouldn't have told him anything. She's my friend and confidant.

To distract myself and maybe him too, I open the trunk of my car and start lifting out bags. With a warm hand on my shoulder, he guides me out of the way and takes the bags from me along with all the others in the trunk.

"You don't have to-" my words are cut off with a growl from him.

I giggle, something I've never really done. "Thanks," I say, earning yet another growl. It's then I remember him telling me I never have to thank him last night. My cheeks heat with a blush.

I lead him into my house and through to the kitchen, thankful that I cleaned it up before leaving.

Not that it was a mess, but it always feels better knowing everything is sparkly clean when you have company over.

Coop surprises me when he starts unpacking the bags of groceries, putting my ice cream in the freezer. We put things away in companionable silence. Once the last bag is empty, he turns to me and I know the inquisition is about to start.

"How are you?" he asks.

I chew on my lip, abusing it further as I consider how to respond.

CHAPTER FOUR

Cooper

My cock hardens behind my zipper at the adorable blush on Mel's cheeks. Not to mention the plump lip she's got trapped between her teeth. I want to rescue that lip with my mouth and kiss away the sting of her teeth. I want to kiss her breathless. I know I need to approach her cautiously, but the desire to rush headlong into this thing is tempting.

"Good?" she answers like it's a question.

"Are you really?" I ask with a raised brow.

She nods. "Yeah, really. I have to admit, I am still curious about, well, everything that happened last night."

I'm taken a little off-guard at her bold statement. I half expected her to shy away from this conversation. "You can ask me anything, kitten."

"How does it work?" she asks boldly.

"It's different for everyone. There are a lot of different kinds of daddy doms and littles."

"What kinds?"

I swallow thickly, getting turned on by such a simple conversation is beneath me, really. It's just being so close to Mel and her sweet honeysuckle scent. "Well, there are those people who participate in age play. The little's regress to a different age and sometimes all the way to baby age. The daddies and even mommies like to take care of them and nurture them and their regressed ages."

Mel scrunches up her nose, telling me that is definitely not something she is interested in, which makes me happy to no end because I'm not one to be into age play either.

"Then there are brats—that one is pretty self-explanatory—you have babygirls who are sweet and total pleasers. Really, there aren't any rules. You can be whatever you want to be. Some are a little bit of everything. It's all about doing what feels right and what makes you happy."

"What about you? What kind of daddy are you?" she asks with an edge of boldness, but her words are laced with shyness.

My already thickening cock hardens to full mast at the question. My kitten wants to know what kind of daddy dom I am. Is it too much to hope that she's curious because she wants to explore this new world with me?

"I like good little girls who like to be punished even if they haven't misbehaved. I like to spoil and pamper my babygirl."

Mel's eyes dilate, and she licks her lips. Her breath shudders from between parted lips. She's turned on by my words. Definitely promising.

"Oh... that sounds..." She tucks her hair behind her ear and shifts on her feet, showing her nerves.

"It sounds?" I prompt, desperate to know her answer.

"Amazing. Your girlfriend must love it."

Is that jealousy I hear? *No need for jealousy, little kitten*, I think to myself.

"I don't have a girlfriend."

"You don't? Why not? That's crazy. You're..." she waves her hands up and down my body.

"I'm what?" I ask, not really expecting an answer. I know I'm pushing her hard, but I can't seem to help it.

"You're you. All fit and hot. I mean, look at you," she sputters.

I chuckle. "I'm certainly me."

She shakes her head. "I just don't understand how you're single. I saw all those women at the club last night. I saw how they look at you." She sounds totally flabbergasted.

"I could ask you the same thing." I raise a brow.

She scoffs. "I'm not a troll or anything, but I'm totally not on your level of hotness."

"I'm waiting for the woman I want to be ready for me," I say honestly.

It's my turn to look her up and down with desire. I admire her curves that she usually hides under her long skirts and dresses. The pants she's wearing right now cling to her curves like a second skin. Her shirt is hanging off one shoulder, exposing the long line of her neck. I want to kiss and taste her skin.

I want to tease her until she's moaning and begging me for more. I close my eyes and take a steadying breath. Not yet. Now is not the time.

"Who?" she asks, seeming agitated at the thought of what my answer will be.

"I don't think you're ready to hear that answer just yet."

She blushes bright pink. Instead of pushing for an answer, she changes the subject back to the club. "What happens at the club?" she asks bravely, almost brazen.

"Want me to show you my curious kitten?"

For a moment, I think she's going to say no and will lose all the bravery she's mustered up to speak so openly with me. She licks her lips hesitating— thinking. I like that she's weighing her options and not just diving into something recklessly no matter how much I want her to say yes. It's good that she's taking her time.

She continues to chew on her bottom lip as she

shifts on her feet. I can see the no on her lips, but the yearning in her eyes screams 'yes.'

"It will be a tour," I say, easing her worries. "Nothing will happen that you don't want to happen. Everything at the club is consensual. They even have monitors who watch and protect the club members."

She nods, acknowledging my words, but I can still see her waffling with indecision.

"Do you trust me?" I ask.

"Yes," she responds with zero hesitation.

"Then trust me, Melinda. I won't let anything happen to you."

She gives me a shy smile. "Okay, yes. I do trust you."

"Tonight," I say, deciding I don't want to give her any time to back down or change her mind. "I'll pick you up and six."

I drop a chaste kiss to the top of her head, then let myself out.

CHAPTER FIVE

Melinda

THE FEELING of the press of Coop's lips on me lingers long after he's gone. It takes me a while to realize what I've agreed to. It's Sunday. I should be finishing my laundry, watching baking shows while reading one of my naughty romance books. I definitely shouldn't be living one of my naughty romances.

It seems crazy to know that I'll be living the life of one of my favorite heroines before long. Panic flares at that thought. What on earth did I agree to? With Cooper Crane, nonetheless. The man I've crushed on for years is going to take me to a BDSM club and show me around.

How is this my life?

My mind decides that answering that question is way too complicated. Instead, it moves right along to stressing about what to wear tonight. It's then I realize that Coop saw me in my sloppy Sunday clothes. Embarrassment burns through me, but then I remember the way he looked at me, and warmth replaces the embarrassment. He looked at me like he wanted to eat me up more than once. Surely he didn't find anything wrong with my outfit.

Now, what do I wear to a sex club? I saw what everyone else wore last night, but none of that is me. I can't even see myself wearing something so provocative. I'm blushing at the very thought of myself in such skimpy clothes.

I take a deep breath and do something I rarely ever do—send a text to Darlene.

Help! What do I wear to the club? Coop is taking me tonight!

Her reply is almost instant. *He is? Yay! Just wear something comfortable.*

Ugh. That's no help. My regular clothes are comfortable, and I felt so out of place last night it wasn't funny. I dig through my closet, pushing aside all of my dresses and skirts. My typical attire isn't at all what someone would wear to a club like The Playground. Or any club for that matter. I finally land on the few pairs of jeans I have in the back of my closet and pull out a dark skinny pair, then find a pretty pink blouse to go with it. It's not fancy, but I'm comfortable and feel pretty. I decide to put on a light coating of mascara and some lip gloss. I'm not a big makeup wearer, but a little can go a long way to making a girl feel good about herself.

The day seems to both drag on and speed by at the same time. By five thirty, my nerves are shot. Thankfully at six on the dot, my doorbell rings. I open the door without even checking to see who it is. I'm so on edge, and my mind is hardly on safety.

"You need to check to see who is at the door," Coop growls. "It's not safe to just open the door like that."

"Sorry. I normally do. I'm just excited," I confess with a blush.

"It's okay, kitten. Just be more careful next time."

I nod my head, lacing my fingers in front of me as I try to hide a little of my exuberance.

Cooper's eyes rove over me, and he licks his lips. "You look amazing," he growls, low and sexy.

I feel flushed and pleased by his compliment. "Thanks. Is this okay? I asked Darlene, and she said to just pick something comfortable."

He reaches out and pulls me close and brushes his lips lightly on mine. "You're perfect."

"Thanks," I breathe against his lips.

He leads me out of the house, giving me a moment to lock up before he's guiding me to his truck. Just like last night, he helps me inside and buckles my belt. This time I don't argue and don't thank him, I just smile happily at his careful treatment.

The drive starts out quiet as dozens of questions flit through my mind, and none of them are about the club. Cooper thinks I look perfect. He kissed me. Is this a date? Or just two friends going to a club? He kissed me!

"What are you thinking about so hard over there?" he asks.

My first knee-jerk reaction is to come up with something on the fly and hide my actual thoughts. Then I remember we are on our way to a sex club. If I can't be translucent about my thoughts right now, when can I be?

"You kissed me."

"I did," he answers plainly.

"Why?"

"Because you're irresistible, kitten."

"Oh..." I say stupidly, my fingers touching my lips as if I could hold his kiss there forever.

"Did you not like it?" he asks.

I blush. "I really liked it. Too much probably," I whisper.

"There's no such thing as too much when it comes to us."

I'm not sure what to say to that. I'm saved from having to respond when we pull into the parking lot of the club. He helps me from the truck, this time lifting me out and letting my body slide down his. I shiver with desire at the touch of his hard body against my softer one. It's like this whole night is building up to the biggest tease ever. First the kiss, now this seemingly innocent touch.

He grasps my hand, threading his fingers through mine as he leads me into the club. The same woman from last night lets us inside. I take in the club through knowing eyes. The shellshock from last night is gone.

"Let's start over here," he says, guiding me towards the almost empty seating area I walked past last night on my way to the bar.

The club seems a lot less busy than last night. Probably because it's a Sunday. I wonder if that's why he decided to show me around today? If so, it's very thoughtful so that I don't get overwhelmed.

"This is a meeting area of sorts," he explains. "Mostly singles come and hang out here to let people know they are looking for a play partner for the evening."

He doesn't linger long and leads me to the bar, which I'm already acquainted with. He points out a doorway I didn't notice last night, explaining it's a second entrance to the restaurant we ate at last night. Knowing that the restaurant is an extension of the club makes sense.

"I wondered about how provocatively everyone was dressed last night. No wonder. It makes so much sense now. I wish I had known before though, I felt so out of place."

Coop turns to face me. "You never have to feel about of place here. That's the point of this club. It's a safe space for everyone."

"My normal clothes aren't really something that fits in here."

"You look beautiful in anything you wear. There's no dress code. You can wear whatever makes you comfortable and feel good."

I nod but don't say anything. I'm honestly not sure how to respond. He called me beautiful. That one word is a whole lot to unpack.

The next area he leads me to looks like a toy store threw up. It's every child's dream come true. "This is where littles can come to play with each other or with their daddies."

I look at every station curiously but feel zero pull to any of the toys. I have read a lot of books with littles who play with toys, but when faced with it in reality, it does nothing for me.

"Do you want to explore?" he asks, motioning towards the play area.

I shake my head. "No, thank you. This doesn't appeal to me at all."

He puts his hand on my lower back and leads me to the next area. My eyes widen as I take in all the BDSM equipment that I've only read about.

"This is the punishment area. Well, and play of a different kind." He winks at me slyly.

I swallow thickly and blush when I notice a woman standing in one of the partitions that look like corners. Her skirt is rucked up around her waist, her red bottom is on full display. My core clenches at the sight. I hardly notice the man in leather pants sitting to the side with elbows on knees and chin rested on his tented fingers. He's obviously watching over his submissive which makes me feel strange.

My skin feels like it's too tight for my body. My imagination runs away with itself as I think of myself in her position. Instead of her spanked bottom on display, it's my spanked bottom. I'd stand there with tears in my eyes feeling thoroughly chastised and contrite for whatever offense I committed.

"Do you like what you see?" Coop rumbles in my ear.

Part of me wants to deny it. I shouldn't like seeing some stranger's butt, and yet... that other part of me wants to experience it for myself.

Once again, I decide to go with blunt honesty. "Yes... I think I do."

He leans in even closer. His lips brush my ear as he speaks, "Does the thought of being punished turn you on? Or is it the idea of being on display for everyone to see what a naughty girl you are?"

I groan my pussy clenching and soaking my panties at the dirty picture he's painting. It's totally both. I never thought I'd be turned on by the idea of being on display. In fact, I think I shouldn't be feeling anything like this. I'm a virgin for crying out loud. I'm definitely not feeling like the shy virgin right now.

Not in the slightest.

I'm hot and needy. Turned on more than I've ever been before. Ready to climb Cooper like a tree and kiss him senseless. Thoughts that I never would've conceived of before last night are running rampant in my mind. My imagination has gone completely bonkers.

"Both... definitely both," I admit breathlessly.

CHAPTER SIX

Cooper

AFTER SHOWING Mel the punishment area, I turn her attention to the club's centerpiece and what gave it its name, the playground.

"It's fairly obvious that this is the playground," I say, sweeping my hand to encompass the entire space where littles of every kind let their little selves out to play. Not only those who like age play, but even littles who don't have any desire to revert to younger years have fun here.

Mel giggles at seeing the few people who are playing currently. Once again, I find myself pleased that our tour is happening on the slowest day of the week. Sunday nights can get busy, but not usually this early.

"Do you want to play?" I ask, noting that she's showing some interest.

"Not tonight," she says shyly.

Not tonight. I can't help but hope that her words mean there will be other times in the future that she'll come to the club.

"Okay, let me know if you change your mind." I drop a kiss to the top of her head. I decide to hold off on showing her the private rooms. I don't want to give her the wrong idea after pushing for her trust. Instead I lead her back to the bar so we can sit and talk.

Tessa is at the bar serving another couple when we walk up. She sees first me, then Mel, and smiles welcomingly at her.

"Hey guys, I'll be right with you."

I lift Mel onto a barstool making her gasp adorably. I don't take my own seat, choosing instead to stand protectively beside her. Not that she's in any danger here. It's just me showing my possessiveness to anyone who might dare glance her way.

Tessa walks up with a big smile. "Hey ya, Mel. So good to see you again," she says happily.

"Hi." Mel blushes. I can tell a little of her shyness is sneaking back to the surface. Shyness that she hasn't shown around me tonight. She's been brave and bold. I love that she trusts me enough to show me that side of herself.

"What can I get you?" Tessa asks, not pushing Mel into a conversation which I appreciate. Tessa usually has all the grace of a bull in a china shop when she's curious about something, and I can definitely see the wheels turning when it comes to Mel.

"The usual for me. What would you like, kitten?"

Mel practically melts into her stool at the endearment. As it is, she leans into me slightly, telling me without words that she likes it.

"Can I have a Shirley Temple with extra cherries?"

"Of course, princess. You can have whatever you want."

Tessa quickly makes our drinks, giving Mel triple the cherries stuck on swizzle sticks inside the pink liquid. Mel smiles in delight as she picks up the first stick and pops a cherry into her mouth.

"Thanks, Tessa," she says as she eats another ruby red cherry.

"Anytime, doll," Tessa says before making herself scarce. Usually she would stick around and chat, but she's wisely opted to give us our space.

I let Mel have a few minutes to decompress after her tour of the club. It's a lot to take in for a veteran BDSMer, let alone people who have lived their lives thinking they're vanilla.

Mel eats another cherry; a drop of juice lingers on her plump lip, and I want nothing more than to lick it off. Her pink tongue sweeps out before I can give in to the temptation.

"So, what do you think of the club?"

"Honestly?"

"I always want your honest opinion," I say, slightly scolding her for even thinking about holding back.

"I feel a little like Ariel when she first gets her legs. It's like a whole new world has been opened up to me."

It's been a long time since I've seen The Little Mermaid, but I definitely get the reference.

"Do you have any questions?"

She looks at me like I'm an idiot before she wipes the expression from her face. Of course she has questions. I deserve every bit of that look.

"How do you find a daddy?" she asks, blushing as red as the cherries she's been snacking on. "You know if someone were looking for that kind of thing."

The question knocks me for a loop. I don't have time to respond before she's asking a bevy of questions.

"How does it all work? What do you like? How do I know what I like? Honestly, I have so many questions I don't know where to start."

My cock is as hard as a fucking rock. I've never been so turned on by simple questions before. Hell, I've never been so turned on, period.

"Oh, kitten," I growl. "You don't have to worry about looking for a daddy because I'm right here."

Mel's eyes widen, and her lips part on a gasp. It

takes every bit of my self-control to not fall on her like a starving man. I want to kiss her. I want to touch her lush body. I want to mark her as mine so every motherfucker knows she's all mine. I want to spank her pretty ass for even considering looking anywhere but at me for a daddy.

I want it all.

CHAPTER SEVEN

Melinda

HOLY CRAP. Did I just say all that? Where did this bold version of myself come from? I would normally never ask such a thing, and yet, here I am, asking Coop how to find a daddy dom. Not only that but I asked what he likes!

I have no clue what's gotten into me other than temporary insanity. It's the only explanation. I'm busy internally freaking out when Cooper says the unexpected. With a low, sexy as fuck growl, he tells me that I won't need to look for a daddy because he's right here.

My panties literally melt right off my body in a puddle of desire for the man who now has his big hands on my hips and is stepping between my legs. He's so close I can smell the smoke and wood scent of the alcohol on his breath and the overwhelmingly masculine scent of his cologne.

Without waiting for my response, his lips find mine in a searing hot kiss. The scruff of his chin abrades my skin, adding another layer of pleasure to our first kiss. His tongue teases at my lips, and I open for him. My lips part on a sigh. His tongue delves inside, slicking against mine. My hands fist in his shirt and I pull him closer. He steps between my legs until I can feel him hot and hard against me.

Everyday Melinda is freaking out right now. The Melinda of today is hungry for more. Today's me is opening her mouth and kissing the man of her dreams back with fervor. I moan into his lips when his hands thread through my hair and grip it tightly making sure I can't escape, not that I would ever want to.

When we break apart, we are both gasping for breath. His dark eyes study me for a long moment before he dives back in for another kiss. I rock against his erection wantonly, seeking pleasure that I know only he can give me. He grips my hips keeping me still.

Someone laughs boisterously, dragging me back to the here and now. I pull away, feeling flushed with both desire and embarrassment. I look past Coop and realize no one is paying attention to us. It dawns on me that this is a sex club. While the kiss rocked my world, it is like nothing to the rest of the members. No one even noticed my entire world shifting realities.

I make the decision here and now to let go of all of my inhibitions and to go for what I really want.

"Play with me?" As soon as I utter the words, I want to call them back. I'm a braver version of myself, but that might be a bit too far. "Unless you don't want to..." I quickly add, giving him an out.

"I'm not sure you're ready for that," he growls, looking disappointed.

My pussy clenches at that low, feral sound. Is he right? Am I rushing into something I'm not ready for? Yes, it's fast, but I don't feel rushed or pressured.

"There's only one way to find out," I say, sounding breathless and needy.

Once again, I find myself wondering who I am and where this side of myself came from. I decide I don't really care where it's coming from, just that I like it.

I squeal when Coop lifts me off the stool and sets me down on my feet. "Warn a girl," I giggle, feeling free and happy.

"Next time."

He grips my hand and pulls me through the club. When he slows his steps as we get to the punishment area my pulse spikes. Can I submit to Coop's dominance in a public setting like this? I'm not really sure, and that has me slowing my steps.

He picks up on my resistance and gives me a reassuring smile. He pulls me close and kisses me below my ear. "There's one part of the club I didn't show you..." he pauses to kiss me again, "the private rooms."

My eyes grow big, and my building nervousness melts away. A private room sounds perfect. Coop takes me down a long hallway to the last door on the right. He opens the door and leads me into a masculine room. There's a huge bed that takes up the majority of the space. It's got a sturdy wood frame, and there's matching furniture throughout the room. On one side is an odd-looking chair that I can only imagine the use for.

Coop gives me a chance to look around. My fingertips graze the top of the bedding then he's spinning me around and pressing his lips to mine again in a blazing kiss that stokes the fire between us. I hate it when he pulls away. I want more of his kisses.

"What do you think?"

"I think it's the best part of the tour," I say, leaning in to kiss him again.

He chuckles and kisses me back. This time when he pulls away, I whimper, trying to chase his lips with my own.

"What do you want, kitten?" he asks, scanning my face for my response.

"I don't know," I answer honestly.

"Do you trust me?"

"Yes, Cooper. I trust you implicitly..." I pause for

a moment gathering my courage to say the next word, "daddy."

That word ignites something inside him. His hand digs into my hair, tilting my head exactly where he wants me as he crushes his lips to mine. I moan at his possessive touch, grabbing ahold of his arms and clinging for dear life as he devours me.

I'm so lost in our kisses that I don't realize his deft fingers have unbuttoned my blouse until he's pushing it off of my shoulders. I have a fleeting moment of nerves because no man has ever seen me undressed before. I knew logically that this step would happen; I just didn't realize how vulnerable I would feel standing in front of a man like Cooper in just my bra. I'm currently thanking God that I have a bit of an obsession with pretty underthings.

I don't have time to worry much because his lips are slipping down my throat and to the upper swell of my breasts. My breaths are coming in gusty pants at the sensual feel of his lips and the soft scruff of his beard on my sensitive skin. I can imagine him between my legs... how that soft hair would feel on my thighs as his mouth played with my pussy.

My core clenches at the thought, my panties becoming a wet mess. Coop slowly nips and kisses his way down my stomach until he's kneeling in front of me. He unbuttons my pants and pulls them down oh so slowly, revealing my light blue panties that are a perfect match to my lacy bra. He takes off my shoes, then pulls my jeans the rest of the way off.

Now I'm standing before him in nothing but my bra and panties, feeling totally revealed and on edge. On the edge of pleasure or the edge of freaking out, I'm not sure. Both seem plausible right now. He presses a light kiss to my panties, and I swoon, falling straight on the side of pleasure. That gentle touch soothed whatever nerves were starting to creep in. That small kiss spoke volumes. He likes what he's revealed and finds me attractive. That's more than enough for me.

"You're fucking gorgeous, Melinda."

The sound of my name on his lips is even sexier than the endearments he's been showering me with. It says he knows exactly who he's with and that he wouldn't change anything. I love it.

He stands before me completely dressed, the juxtaposition is a sexy one, but I want to touch him too. I tug at his shirt, wanting to feel his muscular chest. Thankfully he cooperates, helping me pull the tight material up and off; otherwise, I never would have been able to undress him. I reach for the button on his jeans, but he stops me.

"Who is in charge, kitten?" he growls.

"You are, daddy," I groan, loving saying that word almost as much as he likes hearing it.

He goes back to kissing me, soft and slow. I run my hands up and down his chest, enjoying the feel of his muscular build and the smattering of chest hair. I rub against it wishing my bra away so I could feel it on my sensitive nipples. I bet it would feel amazing.

As if he's read my mind, he releases the clasp on my bra and lets it fall to the floor at our feet. His big hands cup my breasts and tease my nipples gently. I gasp and moan, loving having someone else's hands on me for the first time. I have a moment of clarity from my sex haze and wonder if I should tell him I'm a virgin or not, but when his lips encircle one turgid peak, I decide now is not the time.

Later. I'll tell him later.

He sucks first one nipple, then the next, teasing them both until my chest is heaving and my hands are gripping the back of his head, holding him to my breasts.

Holy crap, that feels amazing.

Cooper chuckles against my skin, and I blush. "I said that out loud, didn't I?"

"Yes," he mumbles against my breast, not lifting his head from the pleasure he's inflicting on my breasts.

He pulls off my nipple with a pop. "Are you ready for more?" he growls. "Is your pussy hot and wet for me?"

I nod my head because, oh my God, yes, I'm wet for him.

"Use your words."

"Yes, I'm wet."

"Good girl," he murmurs.

My knees feel weak at those two words. Two words I've imagined being spoken to me a million times since I first found the naughty daddy dom books I love to read. It's even better in reality than it is in my imagination. Everything is better in reality.

His fingers slip down and into my panties, testing my wetness. I shudder as his thick, calloused fingers touch me for the first time. He slips his fingers through my folds, and my knees nearly buckle. He wraps his free arm around me, holding me up. He toys with me, not touching me with any purpose, just touching, teasing.

"Cooper," I moan. "Please."

"Please what?"

"I need more. Don't tease me."

He chuckles darkly. "Teasing is half the fun, babygirl."

He pulls his fingers from my panties and brings them up to his lips, sucking them clean. My pussy clenches when he closes his eyes and makes a low pleased sound in the back of his throat. "Delicious, like cherries."

I blush at that because I know he doesn't realize how close to reality that is. Not that I think virginity tastes like cherries or anything like that; it's just that there is a cherry there for him if he'll take it. Again, I debate telling him about my virginity, but he kisses me again, letting me taste my essence on his lips, and I can't find the words.

The kiss goes on for long moments until I'm dizzy with desire. I gasp when Coop pulls away then spins us, sitting on the bed and pulling me over his knee in one quick motion. His big hand palms my ass, and I clench up, knowing what happens next.

"Are you ready for more?" he growls, massaging my bottom.

"Yesss," I hiss. Equal parts excitement, curiosity, and fear are bouncing around inside me.

He lifts his hand and drops it back down in a light spank. I settle in and relax, trusting that he's not going to hurt me. He lightly swats my ass several times, alternating between cheeks. Then he's rubbing the heat into my skin.

"Okay?" he asks.

"Yes, daddy," I say, loving the thrill of getting to call him that.

Coop squeezes my ass tight in his big palm, then pulls it back and spanks me harder than before. I gasp at the stinging pain, but by the third spank, I'm leaning into the small pain. Just as I'm getting used to it, his fingers slip under my panties, and he teases my core. I blush at the wet sounds his fingers make as they slide through my folds. He swirls around my clit then up to my entrance. He slowly slips one big finger inside me, and I'm moaning like a wanton.

It feels so different having someone else touching me. One thick finger inside me, and I'm ready to come unglued.

"Fuck, babygirl. You're tight."

I swallow back my nerves. "I'm a virgin," I whisper.

He lets out a low groan, and without being able to see his expression, I'm not sure if it's a groan of pleasure or disappointment.

"I'm sorry," I murmur even quieter.

His finger moves inside me again. "Don't ever apologize for being who you are," Coop says harshly, then spanks me harder than before. "You're perfect just like you are. I could never be upset that you saved this pretty little pussy just for daddy."

This time I'm the one groaning because his dirty words are enough to have me clenching around his finger.

"Hm... does my sweet kitten like when I talk dirty to her?"

"Yes, daddy."

"Good girl. I'm going to spank your perfect ass now."

CHAPTER EIGHT

Cooper

I NEVER THOUGHT I'd have Mel in a private room over my knee and ready for a spanking and whatever else my kinky heart desires. Then she softly admits to being a virgin and my already hard cock thickens and leaks precome in my boxers. My sweet girl is a virgin, and I can't wait to pop that cherry and claim it for my own.

But I will wait. I'll wait until it's perfect for her like she deserves. I won't fall on her like a savage animal. No, I'll make it everything she's always dreamed about. She'll be made to feel like a princess... my queen.

I shake away my fantasies and get back to the lovely woman laid over my lap, awaiting her spanking. I bring my palm down harder on her upturned bottom, pulling a sexy moan from her lips. Tired of her panties blocking my view of the color I'm painting on her cheeks, I shove them down below her ass. I groan at the pretty pink blush from my hand.

"Okay?" I ask her gruffly. It's important to check in with her every step of the way. I would never forgive myself if I took it too far the first time she submits to me.

"So good," she groans, lifting her ass silently begging for more.

I run my fingers through her folds again, testing her desire. She's soaked. My finger easily slips into her tight sheathe. I finger her until she's panting and pushing back into my hand. Her moans and the almost frantic way she's moving tell me she's close. I pull away, denying her the release she craves.

She whimpers, then moans when my hand comes down on her ass again and again. The light shade of pink blooms to a darker shade as my hand falls on her pale skin. I love seeing my marks on her. I could come just like this. Her sweet body writhing over my lap, begging me to give her everything.

Mel gasps and moans, moving restlessly. Teasing me further. My focus is torn between the sweet tease from her gorgeous body and the spanking that's causing her to move so seductively on me. I finally manage to move my attention back to my sweet kitten and her upturned ass. I lay out a few more spanks, then slip my fingers back between her folds. I circle her clit until she's crying out and on the verge of coming. I stop before she reaches her climax, but don't leave her pussy.

No, I couldn't stop if I wanted to. I push one finger, then two into her tight cunt. It flutters around my fingers, clenching down, letting me know how close she truly is. I fuck into her, hitting her g-spot with every thrust of my fingers. She's whining and moaning, calling out my name and begging me not to stop.

She's balanced on the precipice, and I crack my hand down on her ass again. Her pussy locks down on my fingers as she comes and comes, soaking my hand. I don't quit fucking her with my fingers as I spank her, dragging out her orgasm.

"Coop! Oh, God. Daddy!" she screams, crying out in a rush of words and babbles.

"That's it, babygirl. Come for me again."

Her pussy grips down on my fingers, and I can only imagine how tight she'd feel around my thick cock. I have to fight back coming in my jeans like a teenager at the way she's writhing over my cock.

I work her through another powerful orgasm, not stopping until she's limp over my lap and making sexy little whining noises that tell me she's completely replete. I lift her up onto my lap and settle her in for a cuddle.

She lets out a sweet little sigh, then giggles. Obviously feeling the high of endorphins that submissives often feel after a scene. She shifts on my lap and gasps as my jeans abrade her freshly spanked ass. I went easy on her. It was just a light spanking, but for someone new to the sensation, it would be even more sensitive than for someone who has been spanked well and often. I simply gave her a taste of what it could be like if she were my babygirl.

Mel welcomed everything perfectly and with enthusiasm. She's exactly what I want in a babygirl, and I'm determined to make her mine now more than ever.

She cuddles into my chest, sighing the sigh of the sated. "That was amazing," she murmurs.

"How are you feeling?" I ask, wanting to make sure she's with me. Though the scene wasn't intense, I feel responsible for ensuring she doesn't experience any regret or worse—sub drop.

"Wonderful," she says languidly. "I feel lighter than I ever have. Is that normal?"

"Yes, it's normal for some submissives. It's part release and part endorphins flooding your system. A lot of subs will experience it. Just relax into it and enjoy."

"Oh," she murmurs, snuggling with her arms wrapped around me. "Do you think I'm a submissive?"

Yes, without a doubt, I think to myself.

"Did you like what we did?" I ask instead.

"Very much," she admits.

"Did you like me taking control?"

"Yes," she sighs happily. "Even when you were being a big meanie and teasing me."

I chuckle at her calling me a meanie. Another time and I might scold her, but today I'm just amused. "I think you're as submissive as I am dominant. The real question is if you want to explore more or if this satisfied your curiosity."

She looks up at me with her dark blue-gray eyes. "I definitely want more. I can't stand the idea that this is it."

My cock twitches at her response. I want to take more now. To show her everything it can be to become my babygirl. She wriggles on my lap, then reaches between us to cup my erection through my jeans. I stop her seeking hand with a groan.

"This isn't about me, kitten."

She wriggles against me again. "What if I want it to be?"

I growl low and menacing. "This is where daddy says 'no,' and you are a good girl and listen."

"What happens if I don't listen?" she asks demurely.

"I'll make your first spanking look like a love tap," I threaten.

"Oh." Her eyes dilate, and she doesn't seem in the least bit put off by the threat. "What happens if I like it?"

I laugh darkly. "There are other punishments, babygirl," I say, licking my lips.

"What kinds of punishments are there?" she asks innocently.

Oh, this is going to be so much fun showing her everything that it means to be a submissive.

"Well, there's writing lines, soap in the mouth, corner time... there are all kinds of fun implements I can spank you with that will certainly not be fun. Daddy can be very creative. A personal favorite of mine is orgasm denial."

"You wouldn't do that to me," she says confidently.

"Oh, babygirl. When you're mine, I'll do everything to you."

She shifts uncomfortably in my lap at the thought. "But that's just cruel."

"All you have to do is be a good girl and you won't have to worry about that." I smirk because I know that she's not going to be a good girl all the time. I have a feeling my girl is going to find her confidence under my guidance, and it'll bring out a whole new side of her.

"I think I've decided to not like spankings," she mutters.

I can't hold back my bark of laughter at that. "We'll see, kitten."

She looks at me hopefully. "Will we?"

"If you want. The decision is yours."

"Yes, I want to explore this with you. I want you to be my daddy."

I groan her words music to my ears. She's so strong, beautiful, and brave. I did nothing deserve her, but I'm not going to give up the opportunity.

"If we do this, we are exclusive," I say.

Mel nods. "I don't want anyone but you, Cooper."

I capture her lips in a searing kiss, sealing her fate with mine.

CHAPTER NINE

Melinda

COOP PULLS UP outside my house and a wave of sadness engulfs me. I hate that this magical night is coming to an end. He gets out of the truck and circles around to help me down. We walk to my front door hand in hand. I turn to him on the porch, I can feel myself pouting, but I can't stop.

He leans in and kisses my lips sweetly. I try to deepen the kiss, but he holds me at bay. I whine and get a swat on my ass for my efforts.

"Don't forget who's in charge here, babygirl."

I gasp and moan at the sharp sting. "You're totally in control, daddy."

"That's right, and tonight I'm kissing my kitten sweetly before sending her inside and to bed."

He pushes his lips back to mine, continuing the sweetness. I sigh into his lips, feeling light and happy. He pulls away but not before dropping a quick kiss to the tip of my nose. It makes me feel giddy that he's taking such tender care of me even in this small way.

"Good night, Melinda. Get some sleep, and I'll see you at school tomorrow."

"Night, Cooper."

I let myself inside, wishing he was coming inside with me. I hate that the night is over. I rest back against the door with a smile on my face. My mind flits over the night. The tour of the club, our talk at the bar, the private room, and everything that happened.

It feels like a dream.

I can't believe I agreed to be Coop's submissive. His babygirl. I'm still wet between my legs and turned on even after the best orgasms of my life. My bottom feels tingly in the best way, and I wonder if there's a handprint there.

How is this my life? I ask myself with a shake of my head. Me. Frumpy and shy Melinda Young has Cooper Crane for a daddy dom. Heck, having a man like Coop being interested in me in the first place is crazy pants. He's so... bold and masculine. He's the quarterback turned football coach. He should be with a leggy cheerleader type, not the band geek. Yet, here we are. He's chosen me. I'm ecstatic.

I run off to the bathroom to check and see if my bottom is red. I push my jeans and panties down and turn to look in the mirror... I'm almost disappointed when I see the barest of pink on my skin. I let out a sad sigh. I like the thought of Cooper's marks on me. Knowing that there is hardly anything to show for my spanking makes me feel a little bereft.

Maybe next time.

I get ready for bed, quickly dressing in my pajamas and cleaning my teeth. It's much later than I normally go to bed, and I will likely be tired in the morning, but it was totally worth it.

My dreams are filled with Cooper and calling him daddy. He spent the night spanking me in the punishment area of the club, then left me to stand in one of the corners just like the woman at the club. I was on display for everyone to see.

I wake up to my alarm feeling wet and horny. I've never been so turned on as I have been the last few days. It can't be normal. Coop has unlocked a wanton inside me. I want everything he has to offer.

I take a quick shower and dress, my thoughts distracted by a conversation we had last night.

"I won't take your virginity tonight, babygirl."

"Why not?" I practically begged. "It's yours."

"Tonight you've had enough firsts. You'll have that first soon enough."

Then he kissed me deeply, making my toes curl.

"Promise, daddy?" I ask.

"Yes," he growled lowly.

Last night I was ready to throw all caution to

the wind, but Cooper was in total control. He knew I wasn't ready even if I didn't. Not that I don't want to have sex with him. No, it's the exact opposite. I want to give him everything and let him give me everything in return.

I fell a little in love with him last night. Most men would've rushed headlong and taken what I have to offer. They would've slaked their lust without a worry about the potential regrets I might've had the next day.

With Cooper, there will be no regrets, but I appreciate his show of control and the proof that not only does he have my best interests at heart, but he's trustworthy too.

I daydream all throughout my breakfast and drive to Thurston Academy, where I'm the band teacher. I park and go straight to my classroom.

A knock at the door makes me jump, my heart thudding in my chest at being startled. I turn, expecting to see Coop, but Darlene is standing there with a huge smile on her face. How did I not see this coming? Oh yeah, I'm completely on Cloud Cooper instead of firmly planted on the ground.

"Tell me everything," Darlene squeals, rushing towards me with that huge smile painted on her pretty face.

"Well, I got a tour of the..." I lower my voice even though we're all alone, "club last night."

"Annnd?" she prompts.

I'm not sure what all Coop would want her to know. We didn't talk about if we would be public or not. What if he wants to keep things between us a secret? I don't want to betray that trust. Plus, I kind of want it to just be for me for a little while. It's not that I don't want to dish everything with my best friend, but I also want to savor the moment for a little longer.

"And it was good," I answer vaguely.

"Are you going back? Was Coop nice? Come on, I'm dying here!" she says rapid fire.

I feel my cheeks heat with a blush at the question about Coop. "He was very good to me. He showed me everything at the club and explained some things. Answered my questions. I'll definitely be going back."

There that was an answer without giving away any of the stuff I want to keep just for myself for now.

"With Cooper?" she asks with her brows raised.

"Yes," I say, giving her a small bone to gnaw on.

Thankfully the bell rings before she can pelt me with more questions. Students start to stream in, officially cutting off all conversation.

"We'll talk more later," she teases.

I slap her arm playfully. "Later."

It's really nice having a girlfriend. I've always been a loner. I was the band geek all throughout high school, much happier with my instruments than being around people. I was too shy in college to step out of my shell. Somehow, Darlene has found a way to coax me out of my shell.

I'm so thankful for that. I don't know what I would do without her.

The first half of the day flies by. When the lunch bell rings, I opt to eat in my classroom instead of the teacher's lounge. I know I can't avoid Darlene for long, but I'm still holding my secrets close to the vest. I make a promise to myself to talk with her soon.

I don't really want to admit to myself that part of the reason I'm avoiding the teacher's lounge is that Cooper might be there. I don't want to risk turning into a shy, blushing virgin again. I'm so unsure how to act around him; it's just easier to avoid him for now.

After I'm finished eating, I grab my favorite guitar and start to play, soothing my nerves with the familiar strings and chords.

The song turns into my favorite, Landslide by Stevie Nicks. First, the chords flow, then the words start spilling from my lips. I sing quietly at first, my voice gaining confidence as the song goes on. The final notes of the song float through the room, leaving me feeling at peace and calm. I didn't realize how wound up I was.

A throat clears behind me, and I jump out of my

seat, almost dropping the guitar. "Sorry, kitten. I didn't mean to startle you."

"It's okay," I say breathlessly, unable to believe that he's here right now when he should be in the teacher's lounge eating his lunch.

"I didn't know you sang..."

I turn thirty shades of pink at that. "I don't sing."

"Bullshit, babygirl. That was amazing."

My cheeks feel so hot I'm surprised I'm not on fire. I'm so embarrassed to have been heard giving in to the music in my heart.

"Don't be embarrassed," he says, closing the distance between us. I set the guitar aside just in time for him to pull me into his arms and kiss me senseless.

I fall into the kiss like he's the only oxygen for a drowning woman... and I'm the one who's drowning. I kiss him back, not even giving a thought to the fact that we are at school and a student or other teacher could walk in at any moment.

He pulls away with teasing flicks of his tongue against mine.

"I've waited all damn day for that," he growls.

"Me too," I breathe, feeling woozy from his touch.

"Did you sleep okay?" he asks, showing once again that his number one concern is me. It's a heady thing.

"Yes, I did. Though it would've been better with you, I think."

He tugs me back against his chest, holding me so close I can feel every rock-hard inch of his muscular body, including the huge erection pressing against my stomach. "Wouldn't have gotten much sleep, kitten."

I giggle at that. "Not sure I would've minded."

CHAPTER TEN

Cooper

MEL FEELS good against my body. I could hold her to me forever if she would let me. I run my hands up and down her curvy body, enjoying the feel of her. She might be wearing a loose dress, but it can't hide her gorgeous body from me.

I slowly raise my hand to cup her cheek and kiss her reverently. She makes a happy noise in the back of her throat, and I deepen the kiss. Our tongues tangle together in this stolen moment.

Regrettably, I pull away. "Will you go out to dinner with me tonight?"

"Of course," she says with a smile. "I'd love to."

"Thank God. I don't think I could have accepted no as an answer."

She giggles. "As if I could say no to you."

I pull her in for another kiss just before the bell rings, and students start coming into the classroom.

"See you after school," I say with a teasing wink. Mel turns a pretty shade of pink.

The day seems to drag on. Knowing that I'm just a short distance from my babygirl and yet I'm unable to see her is driving me to madness. My last class of the day might've gotten the brunt of that frustration in the form of extra drills.

Finally, the last bell of the day tolls and it's time for me to see my girl. I rush the boys out of the locker room so I can lock up and meet Mel at her classroom to walk her to her car.

She's in with a student, so I patiently wait. I breathe a sigh of relief when her student thanks her for her help and leaves. I rush into the room, shutting the door behind me and turning the lock. I don't hesitate to swoop in and grab her around the waist. My lips are hot and heavy on hers in seconds.

With a gasp, she opens her lips and kisses me back with just as much fervor.

"Missed you," I mutter against her lips, kissing her again.

"Me too," she says, pulling away to catch her breath, then she pushes her lips to mine again.

I completely lose myself in her, forgetting everything around us. Our tongues slick against each other, dancing and dueling together. I can't get enough of her. She's perfection and all mine. If I don't stop now, I might never stop, and she definitely deserves more than a quick fuck in her classroom. Which is exactly what my cock wants right now.

With effort, I set her down and push her from my hold. Mel whimpers and tries to step back against me.

"We need to go, babygirl," I groan.

"Yeah," she nods.

My intention is to just give her a quick kiss, but that's not what happens. One second my lips are lightly brushing hers, and the next, we are devouring each other. Mel has her arms wrapped around my neck, clinging to me. My cock is thick and hard behind my zipper, ready for her.

Somehow I'm able to get control of myself again and pull away. "Come on, if we don't leave now, we're going to go too far."

"Okay, let's go."

She says the right thing, but I can tell the last thing she wants to do is stop right now. I help her collect her things, carrying her bag for her. We walk side by side to her car. I help her inside, and she smiles up at me.

"I'll follow you home, then we'll go to dinner in my truck."

"Okay, daddy," she whispers.

I lean in and kiss her. When I straighten up, she's looking around as if she's trying to see if anyone saw me kiss her. Is she just being shy, or does she want to keep our relationship a secret?

"What if someone sees?" she asks.

"Let them see. You're mine, babygirl."

Mel's cheeks turn pink, and her eyes light up happily. "I like that."

"Good, because it's not changing. Drive safe," I say, then shut her car door.

I jog to my truck so I can follow her home. It takes twenty minutes to get to Melinda's house. I pull up to the curb and hop out of my truck. By the time I get to her car, she's already exiting and pulling her bags out of the backseat.

"You should have waited for me," I scold.

"Sorry, I didn't even think."

I take her bags from her hands. "When I'm around, I take care of you, babygirl."

She smiles shyly. "Thank you."

I growl playfully, swatting her bottom. "What did I say about thanking me?"

"Heaven forbid I have good manners," she snarks back, though it has no fire behind it. She's being playful and I love that this side that no one else sees is coming out.

I carry her bags into the house, then quickly tug her out of the house before I give in to the temptation of having a bed so close. I help her into the truck and shut her inside. I adjust my cock in my jeans as I walk around to my side. I can't seem to get control of the bastard. Every minute I'm around her it just gets worse.

She slips her hand into mine on the drive to the restaurant, and I gladly hold her hand. It's nice being close to her in this small way. It's made even better by the small smiles she keeps sending my way.

I pull up to the restaurant and have a moment of worry that she won't like Italian food. "Is Zia's okay?"

She smiles wide. "It sounds amazing. I'm starving."

"We better get you fed then."

We're quickly seated, and the waiter brings us our water and takes our order. The man blatantly flirts with Mel, and I'd be a jealous bastard over it if she even hinted at being aware of the flirtatious man. She doesn't seem to notice his attention. My girl is so sweet and beguiling. I don't understand how she's gone through life without someone snapping her up. Though I'm damn happy for that because I want her for my own.

We spend a few minutes looking over our menus. A quick glance tells me that she's having a hard time deciding. Her brow is furrowed, and her eyes keep flicking back and forth as if she's debating.

"What are you going to get?" I ask.

She studies the menu for a moment longer then shrugs. "It all looks so good," she says with a sigh. "I hate choosing. What if I choose wrong and it ends up not being what I want?"

"I can help with that."

"You can?" she asks skeptically.

"Tell me the top three things that sound good."

"Hmm... the chicken alfredo, the cheese ravioli, and the cheese lasagna."

Her eyes light up when she makes her last choice, letting me know that's what she really wants. She's just hungry and distracted by the other options. Not an unusual problem to have, but definitely one I can easily solve.

The waiter comes and asks if we are ready to order, and without consulting her, I order for us both. "I'll have the chicken parmesan, and she'll have the cheese lasagna."

Mel smiles at my choice and licks her lips as if she can already taste it.

"How'd you know?" she asks, curious as always.

"Daddy superpower," I say with a teasing wink that brings out the giggle that I adore.

Our conversation flows smoothly, and we find out that we have a lot of things in common. Everything seems to be going well for our first official date... that is until I mention this afternoon and her answers become short and stilted.

"So tell me, why don't you sing? You have a beautiful voice."

She pushes her food around her plate, not meeting my eyes, officially closing herself off from me. "The same reason I don't play in public."

"What?" I ask, surprised. "You play for your students all the time. What about when you were in school?"

"I *teach* my students, not play for them. Huge difference. As for back in school, that was different. I was one of two hundred. I barely counted as a drop in the bucket."

She's still pushing her food around and refusing to look at me. I hate hearing her so down on herself. I hate seeing how she's closed off on me even more.

"That's not true, babygirl. You always make more than a drop. You're the whole damn bucket."

"I don't like the attention. I play for myself."

"Well, you should be playing and singing for everyone to hear."

She lets out a bark of laughter like what I've said is the most ridiculous thing she's ever heard. "Never going to happen, Coop. Just drop it, please."

It baffles me that she's locked away such talent, but I drop it. I know when an argument is lost, and this one is most certainly over... for now. It doesn't mean I won't encourage her later. I'm considering this a strategic exit.

The rest of dinner is filled with stories about students and other light topics. Mel is funny and witty. I could talk to her for hours and never get bored and if we didn't have work in the morning, I would.

I drop a few bills on the table and escort her to my truck. I pull up in front of her house and walk her to the door.

"Want to come in?" she asks with a hopeful expression on her beautiful face.

I groan at the temptation. "I very much do." Her eyes light up and she reaches in her bag for her keys. "But... not tonight."

The light in her eyes dims, and she pushes her bottom lip out in a pout. "I'm ready if that's what you're worried about. It's not like I was saving myself for marriage or anything like that. I just hadn't ever... I don't know... connected with anyone before you."

I lean in and plant a kiss on her lips, then tug her against my chest in a hug. "I know you are, kitten. That's not why I can't come in. It's late and we have an early morning. What I want to do to you is going to take time."

Her eyes dilate and her breathing becomes labored. "I don't see a problem with staying up all night. That's what caffeine is for."

"I'd be a poor excuse for daddy if I kept you up all night on a school night."

Mel giggles. "You make me sound like a naughty schoolgirl."

"Mm... Are you naughty?"

"My thoughts are far from pure," she says, gripping me by the waistband of my jeans and tugging me against her lush body.

I tangle my fingers in her hair, tipping her head back. She meets my gaze with lust-filled eyes. I lean in oh so slowly and brush my lips across hers. She tries to press closer. I hold her tight, not letting her move.

"And that's why I'm not coming inside."

"Still don't see a problem..."

"Soon, babygirl," I say before kissing her senseless.

"HEY, COOP. HOW'S IT GOING?" Colt asks as he comes into the weight room where I'm working out.

"Good, man," I say, pushing the heavy bar up again. "How are you?"

"Great. Thought I'd get a workout in before school since I can't seem to stay late these days."

I know just what he means. Every day after school feels like a rush to spend time with Mel. It's both torture and wonderful. Who knew abstaining would be so hard? I've managed to stick to my guns, though when it comes to sex. Mel sure hasn't made it easy though. Every day it gets harder and harder to resist her.

Thank God today is Friday, and we have a date at the club where I've already reserved a private room. I think if we had to wait much longer, we'd both lose our minds.

I work out harder than normal trying to work off some of the pent-up sexual tension I'm feeling, but it's not working. Nothing is going to get me under control except for slaking my lust in my babygirl.

"How's everything with Darlene?" I ask, trying to find a new distraction.

"Good. Great, in fact. Since you asked about Darlene, does that mean I get to ask about Mel?" he teases.

"Things are going really good. Trying to take things slow. Ease her into our world." Colt is a daddy, and Darlene is his babygirl so he understands the importance of taking things slow.

"Darlene said you're going to the club tonight."

"Yep." I don't elaborate, and he doesn't ask for more information.

I mop up the sweat on my face and chest on my discarded shirt and move on to a treadmill. If lifting didn't help, maybe running a few miles will assuage my lustful thoughts. Just one more school day to survive, then tonight Mel is mine in every sense of the word.

Thankfully the day speeds by, and before I know

it, I'm picking Mel up at her house. She opens the door and I'm completely gobsmacked at what I see. Mel's skirt barely hits her knees. Her top is sleeveless and tight, showing off her curves. I've never seen her show so much skin, yet she still looks conservative and completely herself.

After I take her in, I realize she's looking at her feet quietly. It makes me wonder if she's uncomfortable in her outfit, then I start to worry she's changed how she dresses for me.

"You look lovely, babygirl."

She looks up at me with a relieved expression and smiles. "Thanks," she says shyly. "Is this okay?"

"Mel, look at me." She meets my gaze with those wide blue-gray eyes, and my heart melts at the innocence I see reflected back at me. She so much wants to please me, and everyone around her that she doesn't realize just being herself is more than enough. "There is no dress code at the club. You could show up buck naked, and no one would blink. I don't care if you wear this outfit, one of your long dresses, jeans, or those skintight yoga pants that hug your curves like a second skin. You wear what makes you happy and comfortable. Do you feel good wearing this?"

"Yes. I feel... different."

"Different?" I ask, not sure I like the sound of that.

"Different good," she says.

I tug her against my chest and kiss the top of her head. "Good. I don't want you to feel like you need to change. You're perfect just how you are."

She wraps her arms around my waist and hugs me tight. "Thank you for saying that. It means a lot to me."

"How many times do I have to tell you that you never have to thank me?"

"At least a million," she says brightly.

I shake my head laughing. "Ready to go, trouble?"

"Yes, daddy." She smiles, letting herself slip into little space. Some people have trouble letting go, but Mel is a natural. She likes deferring to me. It's a heady thing.

"Let's go, babygirl."

When we get to the club, it's packed. Fridays are always busy. Mel sticks close to my side and seems nervous around so many people. My first instinct is to drag her off to the private room and away from the crowd, but I decide it's better for her to get acclimated to how busy the club can sometimes be. I lead her to the bar, hoping that Tessa is working so that Mel has another friendly face to see.

Tessa is busy with a group of doms at the other end of the bar when we walk up. I get my girl settled on the only free stool and stand sentry beside her. I wrap my arm around her and hold her close. Every minute that passes, she seems to relax, the tension eking out of her.

"Hey, guys!" Tessa says, obviously excited to see us. "What are you up to tonight?"

Mel flushes bright pink because it's no secret what people come to the club for. She knows that we are here for the private rooms.

"We're here to let Mel experience more of the club."

Tessa smiles wide, her bright white teeth flashing beyond her ruby red lipstick. "I'm due for a break in thirty minutes if you want to play, Melinda." She sounds hopeful, almost lonely.

"Not tonight," I say, feeling slightly guilty, but tonight is just for my girl and me. Mel squeezes my hand in silent thanks for my taking the lead. "We've got a different kind of play in mind."

"Oh," Tessa says, her smile falling for a brief moment before she forces it to brighten again. I almost ask what's wrong because Tessa is never down, but she wipes away any trace of sadness like it never existed before I get the chance. "Well, maybe next time."

Mel nods. "Yes. I'd like to take a turn on the playground. I still can't believe it's for grownups."

Both girls laugh. Tessa has to serve other customers and I lean in close to Mel's ear. "Ready to play, babygirl?"

"God, yes," she says, sounding relieved. I have a feeling I could have taken her straight to the private room that I reserved, and she would've been happier than chatting with Tessa.

We quickly walk through the club, not stopping to take in any of the sights even though there are a lot of scenes happening in different areas. She gives me a questioning look when I open the door to the same private room as last time.

"I thought you might like something familiar."

She nods appreciatively, but instantly she looks to the tips of her toes, shyness overcoming her. Not wanting to give her time to fall into her doubts, I take her in my arms and kiss her. The moment our lips touch, the pent-up lust from the week overflows and ignites in a burning inferno of desire.

My hands tug at her clothes, stripping her of her shirt and skirt in seconds. By the time I make quick work of the clasp on her bra, she's only managed to pull off my shirt. I take a step back, admiring the soft curve of her breasts and all the beautiful pale skin I've uncovered.

She shifts on her feet as my gaze peruses her body. Her fingers twitch at her sides, and I get the feeling she wants to cover herself, but she's resisting the urge—such a good girl. I run my hands over her shoulders and down to those twitching fingers. I thread my fingers through hers and look her in the eyes.

"You're stunning, Melinda. Positively stunning."

A blush grows on her chest and up her cheeks. I don't give her the chance to say anything. Instead, I give her mouth something else to do—kiss. Our lips come together in a mating of mouths. Tongues twirl and swirl, slicking against each other. Lips tease and caress. Noses bump, and teeth clash. It's passionate and speaks of things to come.

I kiss down her neck and to one berry pink nipple. I lick the tip causing her to shudder. She gasps as I take it in my mouth, swirling my tongue around the turgid peak.

"Cooper," she moans my name, gripping my shoulders to hold herself steady.

I pull away from her breast and look up at her. She's looking down with heavy-lidded eyes, her desire obvious. "In this room, I'm daddy," I growl against her skin.

"Daddy," she whispers shyly.

"Good girl."

Mel's head falls back on a moan at my praise. I take the opportunity to tease her other nipple. Licking, sucking, and nipping the tender flesh until she's gasping and gripping my shoulders tight. I switch to the other nipple lavishing it with the same attention. Her knees go weak; before she can lose her balance, I lift her from her feet and carry her to the big bed.

I lay her out like a beautiful sacrifice. Naked save for her pale-yellow panties. I crawl up the bed, kissing every inch of her skin from the tips of her toes up until my lips are poised over hers once again.

CHAPTER ELEVEN

Melinda

IT FEELS like his lips are everywhere at once. Kissing, licking, and teasing every inch of my newly exposed skin. He teases my nipples with gentle nips of his teeth and tender licks of his tongue. My knees are weak from pleasure and we haven't even gotten to the good stuff yet.

I'll be honest, I thought since we are at the club, there would be a spanking and that tonight would be about introducing me to some new kinky thing. This tenderness is not what I expected, but I'm beyond pleased. This is everything I dreamed this moment would be and more.

Cooper picks me up, causing me to gasp, and carries me to the bed. That maddening mouth of his teases the tips of my toes with ticklish kisses then moves up to my ankles. I giggle and jerk my feet at the tickling sensations. He slowly makes his way up my body, giving my nipples special attention, then he stretches his body over mine, his lips a hairsbreadth from mine.

"You're fucking perfect," he growls, crashing his lips to mine.

We kiss for what feels like the most amazing eternity. Our hands exploring each other's exposed skin. I could kiss him like this forever. His big body hovering over my smaller frame. His chest hair teasing my nipples as his thick cock rests against my thigh. I've never hated a piece of clothing as much as I hate his jeans right now.

I want to feel him. Hot and hard against my skin. I want to see his thick length and finally know what it's like to touch him.

I've been dreaming about it for days. Literally dreaming about this moment and what it would be like. I can't wait to experience more. Just when I think I might die from needing him, he moves back down, nipping at my chin playfully as those dark eyes of his look at me with unadulterated lust.

"This okay?" he asks, always checking in on me. Something that would frustrate me if it weren't so darn sweet.

"Perfect. More, please," I groan, running my fingers through his hair.

He doesn't hesitate to move down my body. Dropping a kiss between my breasts before fitting himself between my spread thighs. He has my legs thrown over his broad shoulders, mouth poised over my most intimate place. I gasp when he kisses my mound over my panties. When he pushes the silky material aside and kisses me lightly on my bare pussy, I nearly come off the bed.

"Oh God, yesss," I moan.

He tongues my slit making hungry noises that turn me on even more.

"Taste so good, babygirl. Like the sweetest honey."

I blush at his words, but I love them. I apparently love the dirty talk.

"Gonna eat this sweet cunt now."

"Yes, daddy. Please," I practically beg.

He spreads me open with gentle fingers, licking one long swipe up my pussy. He tongues my clit until I'm crying out from the overwhelming pleasure. He backs away, not letting me reach my climax. Before I can complain, he thrusts his tongue inside me. I throw my head back when that devilish tongue enters me, fucking me like it's his cock.

Cooper fucks me with his tongue until I'm writhing on the bed. Again, the evil man pulls away before I come but doesn't torture me for long because he's back at my clit, circling that sensitive bundle of nerves. I groan when he inserts first one thick finger, then a second.

"Fuck, babygirl. You're so tight. So hot. Can't wait to have you wrapped around my cock."

Dirty talk is my new favorite thing, I decide. My pussy clenches down on his fingers, and I feel myself getting even wetter for him.

"Then don't wait," I moan. "Take me, Cooper. I'm all yours."

He lets out a low groan but doesn't move from his spot. He just keeps licking my clit and fucking me with his fingers.

"I don't want to hurt you," he finally admits. I can tell he's on the edge of his self-control. He wants me as bad as I want him. He's just holding back.

"I trust you, daddy."

I gasp when he sucks my clit with more purpose. All teasing has halted as he brings me to the precipice and pushes me straight over the edge into a white-hot orgasm that's so powerful, I scream the building down. Not even caring or giving thought to who hears.

Coop stands from the bed and strips his jeans and boxers in one quick motion. He reaches into his pocket and pulls out a condom before joining me on the bed. I scrunch my nose up, hating the idea of anything between us but knowing it's the responsible thing. Just because it's the right thing doesn't keep me from telling him I'm on birth control. Thank God for horrible irregular periods.

"I'm clean," he says. "I wouldn't do anything to hurt you."

"I know, daddy."

He holds up the condom. "Are you sure?"

"Yes, positive. I want to feel you. All of you."

"God, you're perfect."

He tosses the condom aside and settles between my thighs, his hard cock resting in the cradle of my legs. He slicks the head of his hardness through my folds, teasing my clit before moving lower and notching himself at my entrance.

"Please," I beg, rocking my hips and trying to take him deeper.

He grips my hips and holds me still. "Don't forget who is in charge," he growls.

"Never, daddy."

Finally, he pushes inside in a slow glide that has me stretching around him, my eyes roll back and my lips part on a moan. There's a tiny pinch of pain, but it's nothing compared to the unyielding pleasure of him entering me for the first time. He feels amazing.

When he's buried deep, our bodies completely aligned, he pauses. "You okay?" he asks through gritted teeth. Even now, he's trying to hold himself in check. It's the last thing I want. No, I don't want perfectly controlled Cooper. I want him wild for me. I want him to lose all that hard-won control he has.

"Yes," I wriggle beneath him as much as I can

with him pinning me to the bed. "Please, I need you to move."

Slowly. Oh so slowly, he pulls out then glides back inside just as slow. He sets a slow pace that drives me mad with lust. My fingers grip his shoulders tight, digging my nails into his hard muscles. He doesn't stop his slow pace. Pulling nearly all the way out before sliding back in to the hilt.

Over and over, he fucks me with precise movements.

I claw at his shoulders, scratching down his chest. I tug him down for a kiss. His cock slides in, hitting me so deeply I groan into his mouth. It feels so fucking good. I want more. Need more.

"Please, daddy. Fuck me. Show me what it's like when you lose control." I nip his bottom lip, a tiny punishment for tormenting me. I hate that he's holding back. I want to experience everything there is, and I don't want to wait. "I'm not fragile. I won't break," I promise.

I gasp as he pulls completely out of my pussy then flips me to my stomach all in one quick motion that has my head spinning.

"You want me to fuck you?" he snarls.

"Yes. God, yes."

"Hands and knees," he growls.

When I don't move fast enough, he spanks my ass. I've barely gotten my bearings when he thrusts back inside me. The new position has his thick cock hitting all the right places. His hands grip my hips tight as he fucks me, pulling me back into him as he thrusts forward. He's holding me so hard I'll bruise. I love it.

"This what you wanted? You want it hard and dirty?"

"Yessss," I hiss as he fucks me even harder.

My pussy clenches around him as he pounds into me. The lewd sounds of his cock thrusting into my soaked pussy and the slapping of his hips against my ass fill the room, along with my cries of pleasure and his gruff moans.

It's a cacophony of sounds that turns me on even more. It's like some lustful music that drives me crazy and leaves me wanting.

"Fuck, you're so goddamn tight. Milking my cock so good."

He slaps my ass in a harsh spank bringing another level of excitement to the moment. I claw at the bedding, falling forward as my arms give out. My ass is tilted upward, changing the angle. With every thrust he's hitting my g-spot.

Holy fuck.

"I'm gonna come," I warn.

"Not yet. Hold it," he growls.

I whimper but try to hold on. The incessant need to come grows and grows until I feel like my orgasm will rip me apart when he finally lets me come. He spanks me hard, once, twice, three times, and I can't hold back anymore. I'm going to break apart if he doesn't let me come soon.

He cages me in, his chest to my back. "Come, babygirl," he gruffly commands, giving the permission I need to let go.

My orgasm crashes through me. I cry out and lose my breath. It feels like I'm going to blackout from the exquisite pleasure. Hell, maybe I do blackout for a moment because the next thing I know, Cooper is groaning low, his cock kicking inside me as the hot rush of his come floods my pussy.

Stars dance in front of my eyes as he wrings every bit of pleasure from me. We both collapse to the bed breathless. He tugs me over his chest, so I'm lying limp over his body. He holds me close as we catch our breath.

I let out a happy, content sigh when he starts gently stroking my back. Running his fingertips up and down my spine. I feel languid and on the verge of passing out from the intensity of it all.

It wasn't at all what I thought my first time would be like, but it was absolute perfection.

"You okay?"

I nod my head, still too breathless to speak.

"I wasn't too rough?" he asks, sounding concerned.

I shake my head. "Not at all," I manage to say.

Coop kisses the top of my head and holds me

close. I doze in his arms. It's late when we finally move from the cocoon of the bed. I instantly regret that we have to leave. I don't want to break the spell. I want tonight to last forever.

"I don't want the night to end," I confess as I pull on my clothes.

"Good thing it's not over," he says with a cocky smirk.

I look at him questioningly as I pull my wet panties up, grimacing a little.

"I'm taking you home, but I'm not leaving tonight."

"Oh."

"Is that okay?" he asks with a raised brow.

I close the distance between us and lean up on my tiptoes to kiss him. "Sounds perfect."

I WAKE up with a stretch and a yawn, my body pleasantly sore. Coop reached for me twice more in the night, making love to me like he'd die if he couldn't. I reach to where he fell asleep next to me and find the bed empty. A wave of sadness floods me. I was looking forward to waking up in his arms.

Did he leave without saying anything? He wouldn't do that... Would he? That's not the kind of man he is; that fact is confirmed when I find his shirt abandoned on the floor where we tossed it last night. I pull it on, loving the feel of the well-worn cotton on my naked body and the scent of his skin surrounding me.

I pad on quiet feet down the hallway searching him out. I find him in the kitchen cooking breakfast. I smile wide at seeing him in my kitchen in nothing but his boxers like he belongs. He totally does. I walk up behind him and wrap my arms around his waist, placing a kiss on his back right between his shoulder blades, then rest my cheek against him.

"Morning, beautiful. Did I wake you?"

"No. I'm not very good at sleeping in, even on my days off."

"Me either," he chuckles.

"What are you making?" I ask. "It smells delicious."

"French toast and bacon."

I smack my lips, my stomach growling hungrily. "Sounds fantastic."

He turns in my arms and encircles me in his arms. "How are you? Did I hurt you last night?"

"Hmm..." I murmur, snuggling against him. "Not at all. I'm a little sore, but in a good way."

"Good. I was worried. I was selfish with you last night."

I can't hold back my giggles. "If that was selfish, you can be selfish every night. I think you nearly killed me with the number of orgasms you gave me."

"Good to know," he chuckles. "Why don't you go take a shower, and I'll finish making breakfast?"

I pout up at him. "What if I want to shower with you?"

He gives me one of those smoldering looks of his. "Then I guess I should come wash my babygirl's back."

"And front?" I ask hopefully.

"Oh yeah," he says with a teasing smile and a light slap to my ass.

He quickly turns the burners off and chases me down the hallway to the bathroom. My shower is small, but we make it work. He rubs his hands all over my body, washing every inch. Every swipe of his soapy hands is a delicious tease. I gasp when his hand slips between my legs, and he washes my sensitive pussy.

"Sore?" he asks, giving me a knowing daddy look.

"Just a little sensitive."

He washes my hair, scraping his nails lightly along my scalp. I moan and lean into him. It's almost as good as sex. Okay, maybe not that good, but dang close. I rub my wet body along his, loving the feel of his slick skin against mine. He's long and hard against my lower back. Even though I woke up sated, my nerve endings prickle with awareness, and my pussy grows wet and needy.

I turn and reach for him, but he pulls my hands

away. "I can help with that," I say, trying to be seductive for the first time ever.

"Babygirl, we are in here to get you clean."

"I'm squeaky clean." I get a naughty idea... "We need to get you clean too. Can I wash you?"

I don't wait for his response; I just grab the soap and lather up my hands. I run my soapy hands over his chest, enjoying the feel of his hard muscles under my hands. He may be in his early forties, but he looks better than most men half his age. I turn him so that I can wash his back and gasp at the red lines I see there.

"Oh my God. Did I do that? I'm so sorry..."

He laughs, not sounding one bit sorry. "My kitten has claws, nothing wrong with that."

I blush in embarrassment at my loss of control. I gently kiss each scratch mark. He groans low in his throat at every touch of my lips. Feeling bold and a little naughty, I reach around and grip his cock, giving it a firm stroke.

"What are you doing?" he growls.

"Trying to entice you..."

"Didn't I say no already?" he groans.

"Funny how a no sometimes sounds like a yes."

He spins around and pins me to the shower wall. The cold surface causes me to gasp, but his soft lips on mine pull a moan from me.

"You're playing with fire, babygirl," he says into my lips before kissing me again.

"Burn me," I moan.

Coop flips off the water and throws me over his shoulder. I grip him around the waist, feeling slippery and like I might slide right off his shoulder, but deep in my heart, I know he'd never let me fall. I squeal when he tosses me to the bed. I bounce once, then he flips me to my stomach and pulls me up to my knees.

His hand cracks down on my bottom like a paddle, and I gasp at the sharp sting. Over and over, he spanks me with firm slaps. I'm panting and moaning as the spanking goes on and on, feeling never-ending. By the time his hand stills on my butt and he starts massaging the stinging skin, I'm soaking wet—my desire dripping down my thighs.

His fingers slide through my folds and he lets out a possessive sound before tsking me. "Naughty girl. Getting all wet from her spanking."

"Sorry, daddy," I gasp as he circles his fingers around my clit. "I can't help it."

He leans over my body, touching me everywhere, his hard cock teasing my folds, then he gently kisses the back of my neck. "I'll tell you a secret, kitten," he growls in my ear. "I don't want you to help it. I want you soaked like this for me always."

His words light a fire inside me. I went from a virgin to a complete and utter hornball in less than a day. I want him more than I've ever wanted anything in my life.

I whimper when he pulls away, leaving me feeling bereft. With one quick motion, he flips me to my back. I barely have time to catch my breath before he's entering me. He pushes in to the hilt and I moan at the stretch. I don't think I'll ever get used to the way he feels inside me. I love how big he is over me. How small and cherished I feel as he covers my body. When he thrusts, rolling his hips so he grinds against my clit, I throw my head back on a moan of pure pleasure.

Coop leans in and kisses me. It's a hot, messy kiss that drives me mad with lust. Our tongues stroke over each other in a frantic dance. He bites my bottom lip as he pulls away.

"Is this what you wanted?" he asks, pounding into me.

"Yes! Yes!" I half-moan, half-scream.

He encircles my throat with his big hand, not squeezing, but the threat is there. My orgasm comes without warning. One second I'm enjoying the feel of him stretching me, and the next, my whole world is breaking apart into a million bright shining pieces.

With a groan, Coop buries himself deep inside my pussy and releases. I love the feeling of him coming inside me. I love the closeness of it. I can't imagine sex with him any other way. He covers my body with his, kissing me sweetly as we both come down from our climaxes.

I whimper when he stands from the bed, leaving me exposed to the cold air of the room. He's back in less than a minute with a washcloth. He cleans me between my legs, then pulls me from the bed. I giggle when he tugs his shirt back over my head.

"I like you in my clothes," he says, kissing the tip of my nose. "Now, let's go finish breakfast."

THIS WEEKEND WAS the best ever. Coop stayed until Sunday night. He was hesitant to leave, and I really didn't want him to go. I tossed and turned last night, unable to get comfortable. After just two nights of sleeping in his arms, falling asleep alone was next to impossible. Despite that, I wake up with a smile on my face.

I still can't believe that I live in a world where Cooper Crane is my boyfriend. I get ready for work floating somewhere around cloud nine. My smile widens when I see Cooper standing by his truck, waiting for me.

He comes over and opens my car door. He reaches in and pulls me out of the car. The moment I'm on my feet, his lips are on mine. I gasp into his lips as his tongue delves between mine. Our tongues slick together as we deepen the kiss. I meet his tongue stroke for stroke, loving the reunion with this man I'm falling for so quickly.

There is a woot and a whistle from somewhere behind me, and I pull away. I look around, seeing that it's a couple of football players.

"Get to class, boys!" Cooper barks at them.

I bury my face in his shirt, embarrassed at being caught making out like a high schooler by high schoolers. A week ago, I never would have done such a thing. Now here I am, the queen of PDA and wanting more. Reluctantly we part, and Coop walks me into the building. Since I no longer feel the need to shyly hide out from him, I head to the teacher's lounge for a cup of coffee.

Darlene is at the coffee pot, and in seconds she's pounced on me for details about Coop and me.

"Tell me everything!" she says excitedly.

What do I tell her? How much do I want to share? The giddy part wants to tell everything. I'm so freaking happy. I finally have not only a best friend but a boyfriend to talk to her about. I look around at the crowded room and lean in close to whisper in her ear.

"Coop stayed at my place all weekend."

Darlene squeals quietly. "Tell me more."

"Later," I say, my eyes moving to the people hanging around just waiting for some new tidbit of gossip to spread. No thanks.

"Fine," she grouses. "Today after school? We can get dinner."

"Pizza?" I say with a smirk.

"Pizza it is."

I giggle happily as we part ways. I've never felt like this before, and I hope the feeling lasts forever. Can a person really fall for another so quickly? My crush for Coop has gone from pining for him from afar to not wanting to be out of touching distance in just a few short days. It hardly seems possible that I can feel so much so fast. And yet, here I am... attached and ready for more.

The day goes by quickly. Sadly, I don't have time to see Coop because he had a lunch meeting with his assistant coaches in preparation for the upcoming game, and directly after school, he has football practice.

I'm extremely glad I have plans for dinner with Darlene; otherwise, I might go crazy. We meet at Nino's. Darlene looks like she's ready to explode from the need to hear all about my weekend with Cooper. We quickly find a table to sit at and order a pizza to share and our drinks. As soon as the waitress is out of earshot, Darlene dives in.

"Now tell me everything."

I laugh at her enthusiasm. "I don't even know where to start."

"Hmm... Tell me about the club."

I turn bright red because the club is where I lost my virginity in the most spectacular way. I'm also not sure how much of this part Coop would want me to share. But Darlene is my best friend, and best friends talk about this kind of thing... right?

"We went to the club Friday..."

"Annnd?"

"Coop got us a private room."

She looks even more excited at my revealing that tiny tidbit.

"It was fantastic," I say shyly. "I honestly never knew it could be like that," I lower my voice to barely a whisper, "Sex that is."

She practically swoons in her seat. "And he stayed at your place all weekend?"

"Yes!" That giddiness I've been walking around with comes back with a vengeance and my cheeks hurt from smiling so much. "It was the best weekend of my life."

"So does that mean you're together-together?"

I wrinkle my nose at that question. We didn't really define our relationship as such, but it sure feels like that's what we are. More even when I consider the whole daddy/babygirl thing.

"Well, we didn't really define it as boyfriend-girl-friend, but it feels that way."

Darlene lets out a happy squeal drawing the attention of the other patrons at the restaurant.

"Shh," I admonish.

"Sorry! I'm just so happy for you. I knew you'd be perfect for each other." She looks around making sure no one is listening in. "And the daddy stuff?" she whispers.

I let out a content sigh. "I love it," I answer honestly. "I liked reading about it, but never thought about it as something I could have in real life... so much better in reality."

"And he's good to you?"

"The best."

We eat and chat more about the club.

"I really like Tessa."

Darlene nods. "She's a hoot. Maybe just don't pick up her bratty habits. Whoever she ends up with has a challenge on his hands."

I laugh at that because from what I've seen it's so true. She's a spitfire. "I don't think brattiness will be a problem for me. I can't see myself ever acting like that."

"Me either. You're too good," she says with a smile.

"Maybe a little naughty," I smirk.

My phone dings with a message. I excitedly pull my phone out because there are only two people who message me, and one of them is sitting across from me right now. I let out a happy sigh when I read Coop's message.

Hey babygirl. Missed you today. Want to get dessert after you're done with dinner?

Darlene crooks up an eyebrow. "I think that's

the first time I've ever seen you happy to look at your cellphone."

I giggle and blush. "I guess it's different when you have a reason to be excited about who is messaging you."

I type out a quick message agreeing to get dessert after my dinner is over. I can't wait to see him again.

Our conversation switches from the club and our boyfriends to school. We briefly talk about the big game and the performance the marching band is putting on for halftime. It's a big deal, and I can't help but feel nervous. I have a great group of students this year, but it never fails to make me feel like I'm the one in the spotlight whenever they have a performance.

"It'll be great," Darlene says. "You guys are state champions. You've got no reason to worry about how they will do."

"I know, it's still nerve-wracking." I don't know if I'll ever get used to it. Even if I'm not out on the field, it still feels like it's me out there in front of the crowd.

"Don't stress over it, girl. They're going to be awesome."

We finish up with our pizza, and I excitedly leave to go meet Cooper for dessert... and hopefully some more of his drugging kisses.

CHAPTER TWELVE

Cooper

AFTER SPENDING the entire weekend with Mel having to go back to reality stinks. It especially sucks to not be able to spend much time together after school hours. Lunches in the teacher's lounge just aren't enough. Stolen kisses in the parking lot really aren't working for me. I'm greedy for her time and attention.

I watch her with hungry eyes as she instructs the marching band at the other end of the field. She's in her element barking orders and ensuring that everything is running smoothly for the big game tomorrow night against our rival team.

The Jaguars and the Eagles have a long-standing rivalry, and this year we are determined to take them down. After last year when they stole the win from us by practically disabling our quarterback, we are ready for revenge. This year the team is pumped and ready for tomorrow and their long-awaited payback.

My attention is once again drawn away from my team's practice and to Mel. She's in one of her typical long skirts, and yet she makes it look like the sexiest lingerie. Or maybe that's just my obsession with her talking.

Practice finally wraps up, and the guys head into the locker room to hit the showers. I saunter over to where the band is still practicing. Mel is like a tiny drill sergeant making sure her band is spot on for every movement of their bodies and every note from their instruments.

I watch her, hungry for her kisses.

She turns, spotting me watching. Her lips tip up on a smile and her cheeks turn pink with the prettiest blush. Finally happy with the band's performance, she dismisses them, thanking them for their hard work. She might be hard on them, but she also makes them feel valued.

The band scatters and Mel walks towards me, meeting me halfway. I can see the same need reflected in her eyes, but she somehow manages to keep distance between us until we get to the bleachers, where we are hidden from view. As soon as we are out of sight of the students, she jumps on me. Her arms go around my neck, and her pouty lips crush to mine. The kiss is instantly wild and untamed. Like always, when we touch, we catch fire.

My hands find her ass and I squeeze. If she weren't wearing such a long skirt, I'd have her legs wrapped around me and her cunt pressed against my hard cock.

I don't care that anyone could walk up at any time; it's been too long since I've had her. I pull back slightly. "Taking you home, babygirl. Need you so bad."

"Yes, daddy."

We grab our belongings as quick as possible and are in my truck heading to her place. It's the longest twenty-minute drive of my life.

We barely make it inside before we are on each other. Greedy hands strip off our clothes as our lips crash together. The second her lush curves are revealed, I fall on her. My lips find the hard peaks of her nipples and her head drops back on a moan. I suck and lick at her sensitive tips, nipping them with my teeth.

Her hands are buried in my hair, tugging at the strands. She whimpers and begs me for more. "Please, daddy."

I kneel in front of her and lift one of her long legs over my shoulder and dive right into her hot pussy. I lick her clit and fuck her with my tongue. I hold her steady as her knees go weak. She buries her hands in my hair, holding me to her pussy.

"Oh, God! I'm gonna come!" she cries out her pleasure.

I redouble my efforts wanting to taste her sweet release. She comes a moment later. Her pussy spasms around my tongue as she falls over the edge. She leans heavily against the wall as she catches her breath. I stand and lift her into my arms and enter her in one quick thrust.

She claws at my shoulders and I love the slight pain that proves she's lost in the moment. That I'm pleasing her so much that she can't control herself.

"Fuck, kitten. You feel so damn good."

"So do you, daddy. So hot and hard inside me. More," she begs.

I thrust into her harder, one hand on the wall behind us, the other on her tight ass holding her to me as we lose ourselves. Mel's pussy clenches down on me as she gets closer and closer to her release.

"You gonna come on my cock?" I growl, knowing how much she likes dirty talk.

"Yesss..." she hisses, digging her nails into me harder.

My balls draw up and my spine tingles as my release nears. I reach between us and rub her clit. She lets out a little scream as she comes, her pussy locking down on me and pulling me over the edge with her. I bury myself deep. My come emptying inside her.

I lean heavily against the wall, pinning her against it as I catch my breath.

"Needed that," she whispers. "I've missed being close to you."

"Me too, babygirl."

I kiss her sweet and slow. Our tongues dance together, none of the previous urgency in our kiss, but it's no less passionate. I carry her to the couch and relax with her in my arms. I hold her close, loving the feel of her against me.

After several long minutes of cuddling, I ask her if she'd like to go get dinner.

"I can cook," she says shyly.

We cook chicken alfredo together. The moment one of domestic bliss. I can see this being my life. Our future. Coming home with Mel and spending the evenings making love and doing simple domestic things together. It would be perfection.

We eat dinner in the living room and watch a movie. We clean up the kitchen together, another moment of domestic bliss as she washes the dishes and I dry. Time seems to fly by, and before long, it's late and time for me to go home.

"Do you have to go?"

"Yes. You need to get your rest, and if I stay, there will be very little resting."

She pouts. "I'm not seeing the problem with that. What if I promise to behave?"

I give her a suspicious look.

"I will be a good girl," she promises.

I do have spare clothes in my truck for the days

I work out. Staying would make me happier than anything. Falling asleep with her in my arms sounds like the best idea ever.

"Let me grab my gym bag from my truck."

"Yay!" she says with a squeal and a little bounce.

Mel looks so happy that I'm pleased with my decision. I always want her to look at me with that happy smile. I fall asleep with her in my arms and it feels perfect.

I WAKE up with Mel in my arms. Definitely the best way to wake up. I slip from the bed and quickly shower and dress. I lean over her on the bed and kiss her awake.

"Time to wake up, beautiful girl."

She stretches and smiles. "I could get used to waking up this way."

"I could get used to waking you up this way," I growl, giving her another kiss.

"I've got to go. We've got one final strategizing meeting this morning before the big game tonight."

She nods. "Okay, daddy. Good luck."

"Thanks, babygirl. I'll see you at school."

Unfortunately, the day ends up being too busy to sneak away to spend time with Mel. Before I know it, we are on the field and my team is cleaning up the field with the Jaguars. The band is set up in the bleachers on the sidelines, waiting for their chance on the field. Mel must feel my eyes on her because she glances up at me with a shy smile before looking back at the students awaiting their performance.

The first half of the game goes well. The Jaguars haven't scored, and we've got two touchdowns. At halftime the team heads into the locker rooms with the assistant coaches hot on their heels. I stick around to watch the band start their performance.

Mel's band is spot on and shows the town once again why they win every competition they enter. I'm so proud of my girl and what she's accomplished in the last three years. Our band went from a rag-tag group of kids who couldn't march for shit to the number one marching band in the state.

I drag myself away from the performance and head towards the locker rooms where my team is waiting for me to give them a pep talk and congratulate them on a fantastic first half. It's my job to encourage them to keep it up for the second half.

"Cooper Crane, as I live and breathe," a nasally voice that I'd recognize anywhere as Janice Lin, a woman I dated a few years back. She's a member of The Playground. How could I forget that she's the cheer coach for the Jaguars?

"Janice."

"What are you up to these days?" she asks, trying to sound sultry but failing.

I take in her willowy frame and can't see what I

ever saw in her. It might've only been a few dates at the club, but that was enough to know she's trouble and was never right for me. Now with Mel in my life, I have zero desire to even talk with this woman.

"I haven't seen you at the club lately," she purrs, coming in close to me. I take a step back, not wanting her to touch me. "I've missed you, daddy," she says, trying to sound seductive and needy.

"I'm not your daddy," I growl, my voice low and dark with my building frustration.

The passage gets more and more crowded as people head to the concessions stand and restrooms. A particularly rowdy group of kids bumps into Janice sending her straight into my arms and exactly where she wanted to be from the start.

Her hands run up and down my chest with a little purr in the back of her throat. "You sure haven't changed."

I grip her wrists in one of my hands, holding her away from touching me. Janice lets out a little gasp and pushes even closer to me. She's jostled again by the crowd, and I grunt in disapproval. Just before I can shout at the rowdy teens, Janice stands on her tiptoes and presses her lips to mine. I'm seconds away from pushing her away, not giving a shit if she lands square on her ass when I hear a gasp.

Somehow through the din of voices, I hear it and know without looking that my sweet girl just saw Janice's lips on mine. My eyes zero in on her and my heart breaks at the look on her face. She looks crushed, tears swimming in her eyes as she takes in the scene in front of her obviously misconstruing it.

Of course she would. The evidence of Janice practically wrapped in my arms, her lips on mine is damning. Mel turns from me and rushes through the crowd. Not even a second passes before I have Janice shoved to the side and I'm chasing after my babygirl.

Mel's short stature works against me as she disappears in the crowd of people. I'm only a few steps behind her, but I still lose sight of her. I spend long minutes searching everywhere for her, but I can't find her. She's gone, and I can't chase after her because the game is resuming, and I can't let my team down. Not during the biggest game of the season. Not when the stands are filled with recruiters and the boys' futures hang in the balance.

I kick a discarded bottle of water, cursing. I run my hands through my hair, tugging at the strands, hating that my girl is out there somewhere hurting, and I can't help ease that pain right now. I'm letting her down, something I swore I would never do. The team is on the field, but my mind is a million miles away.

I pull out my phone and send a text to Mel, the only thing I can do right now even though it's a poor excuse of contact.

It's not what it looked like. I swear to you, babygirl. Please come back and talk to me.

I stare at my phone, hoping that I'll see the bouncing dots that tell me she's read my message and is responding, but my phone is silent. I check my damn phone at least a million times during the second half of the game, cursing Janice every time when I see there's no response from Mel.

Finally the game ends with a win. Despite my distraction, the guys pulled off a total shutout. I'm so damn proud of them but can't feel the excitement knowing that somewhere out there, my Melinda is thinking the worst of me.

I congratulate the team but don't stick around to celebrate. How could I when I've got a woman to find and a relationship to fix. There is no way I'm letting Janice Lin get in the way of my relationship with Melinda. I would rather die than lose her, as dramatic as that sounds. I rush out of the stadium and to my truck. I peel out of the parking lot, driving like a madman to Melinda's house.

My heart sinks when I pull up outside and realize her car isn't in the driveway and the house is completely dark. She didn't come home. Where did she go? My worry grows as I sit outside her house waiting for her to show up. I pull out my phone and call her. It rings off to voicemail after several unanswered rings.

"You've reached Melinda Young; leave a message

at the beep." I smile at the formality in her message. It's just like my Mel and it makes my heart clench in my chest. The line beeps and I'm tongue-tied for a moment.

"Mel, baby, please listen to me... what you saw isn't what it looked like. I swear to you. Please come home. I'm waiting for you. I-" The words 'I love you' are on the tip of my tongue, but I bite them back. Now isn't the time to declare my love. Not when I've just broken her heart. I won't manipulate her like that. She deserves to hear the words in a sweet moment, not when I'm begging for my life. "Call me... please."

I sit outside her house for over an hour like a fucking stalker, not giving a shit when the neighbors give me suspicious glances. I refuse to leave until I've talked to Melinda. Nothing will get me out of this truck until she's home.

I finally give in and dial Colt. Maybe Darlene has heard from Mel, and they can tell me where she went. The phone only rings twice before Colt answers. I don't wait for niceties before I dive in with my questions.

"Have you or Darlene heard from Mel?"

"I haven't... Let me ask Darlene." He speaks quietly away from the phone for a moment then he's back. "Darlene hasn't heard from her. Why what's wrong?"

I let out a frustrated sigh and run my hand

through my hair again, tugging at the ends. "Fucking Janice showed up at the game tonight. I mean, of course she did; she's the Jaguar's cheer coach. She caught me off guard. Man, she fucking kissed me, and Mel saw it."

"Oh fuck, brother," Colt says with sympathy.

"I know. I tried to chase after her, but she took off before I could get to her. I should've left the game... I just couldn't disappoint the guys." I swipe a hand down my face, feeling tired and so, so filled with regret.

"I'll let you know if I hear from her..." He pauses for a moment, and I can hear Darlene's soft voice in the background. "I might only be able to tell you she's okay... Darlene won't let me betray her friendship if Mel doesn't want to be found."

I let out a frustrated sound, but I understand. I wouldn't want Darlene to betray her... not when she already thinks that one person she cares for has betrayed her.

"Thanks, man."

"You're welcome. Hang in there."

I sit outside Mel's house long into the night. Finally, around three, I give up and head home. She's obviously staying elsewhere and being here isn't helping anything.

CHAPTER THIRTEEN

Melinda

WITH A BROKEN HEART, I check into a hotel. The desk clerk gives me a weird look. I'm guessing they don't get many people checking in without luggage. Or maybe it's my red-rimmed and puffy eyes that have him looking at me like that.

My phone rings again, and I once again ignore it. Coop has called at least ten times since the game ended. Maybe I should've stuck around for him to explain things, but my fight or flight instincts kicked in, and flight won hands down. I'm definitely at the hide and lick my wounds stage of things.

Maybe I'll feel more like talking in the morning... or maybe not, I think as my brain conjures up the image of that woman's lips pressed against my man's. It breaks my heart all over again, and I can feel another round of tears pooling in my eyes. The attendant hands me my key card, and I rush away. I don't want to cry in public, at least not again. It's bad enough that half of my students saw me crying as I pushed my way through the crowd at the game as I escaped to my car.

By some miracle, I make it to my room before the tears start falling. I don't even take a moment to look around the room before I throw myself down on the bed and pull one of the fluffy pillows to my chest. I curl around it and let my heartache flow freely.

How could I let this happen? I jumped into this thing with Cooper with both feet and zero reservations. Look what happened. I ignored my cautious side; now I'm paying for it. It was impossible to hold back with Coop. Not when he was giving me everything I ever dreamed of. Not when he made my deepest fantasies come to life.

Another sob bubbles to the surface and I lose myself in my grief. I cry and cry until I eventually fall asleep. My dreams are plagued with the sight of the beautiful woman wrapped around Cooper. Both of them laughing at the frumpy little band teacher and her stupid little crush.

I wake up much too early, eyes swollen and feeling even worse than I did last night. I stumble bleary-eyed to the bathroom and turn on the shower, hoping that the water will cleanse me of my emotions. The hot water feels good, yet I don't feel any better. I stay under the spray until my skin is red from the heat of it. By the time I turn off the water, I feel drained completely.

Showers always refresh and rejuvenate me, but this one sucked the life out of me. Or maybe that's just my broken heart. I wrap up in the fluffy hotel robe and wander back into the main room. I notice for the first time how nice the room is. I open the curtains and am met with a view of the river that flows on the outskirts of town.

After a deep, cleansing breath, I decide to order room service. Despite my emotions, I'm starving. I order pancakes... the perfect food for a broken-hearted fool. I've just sat down to eat when my phone rings. I cringe, hating the thought of talking to Cooper when I'm still so raw, but I can't hide out forever.

It's now or never, I think to myself. Never sounds awful good right about now.

I nearly drop from relief when I see Darlene's name on the little screen instead of Cooper's, then I instantly feel regret because I realize I really do want to speak with him. He hasn't tried to reach out yet today... has he given up already?

My heart breaks a little more at that thought.

With a bracing breath, I answer the phone. Darlene barely lets me get out my hello before she starts talking.

"Girl, where are you? I've been worried sick after Coop called last night looking for you."

"Sorry," I say, feeling like a horrible friend for making her worry. Though at the same time, it feels good knowing there is someone out there who cares enough to worry. "I didn't mean to make you worry. I just…" I trail off with a sniffle as my eyes fill with tears again.

"It's okay," Darlene says, consoling me. "I understand. I've been there before, trust me."

And I know she's telling the truth. I remember her brief break-up with Colt and how it wrecked her. Though her man was faithful so I'm not sure that it's exactly the same feeling of heartache.

"I still hate that I made you worry." I sniffle again, hating that I can't seem to stop crying now that I'm talking to my best friend.

"Where are you, doll?" she asks, letting sympathy flow through her words.

"I'm at the Sunbreak Hotel. I couldn't bear to go home, knowing that's the first place Coop would look for me. I just… I can't right now. I'm too raw to even talk to him."

"I understand. I truly do. Want me to come over?"

My eyes well with even more tears at her offer. Part of me wants to be alone forever. The other part wants her best friend. "Yes, please."

I give her my room number and we hang up. I pull on my clothes from yesterday, hating that I'm wearing the same clothes again. I feel scummy and unclean, but I don't have another option right now.

Thirty minutes later, there is a soft knock on my door. I check the peephole and feel a little bit of relief when I see Darlene standing on the other side. I open the door and burst into tears.

"Oh, honey," she says, pulling me into a hug and walking me back into the room so she can shut the door. "It's okay."

"N-no, it's n-not," I stutter through my tears. And it really isn't. Nothing in my life is okay right now.

Darlene walks me to the end of the bed and sits down with me still wrapped in her arms. "Okay, it might not be okay right this second, but it will be okay. This I promise."

I pull away, looking at her through my tears. "How can you be so sure?"

Darlene shrugs, looking chagrined. "I'm not. It just seemed like the right thing to say."

"That's less than helpful."

She nods in agreement. "Why don't you tell me what happened, and we can go from there on whether or not things will be okay?"

I sigh heavily but resign myself to telling her what I saw.

"I finished up the half-time show and wanted to congratulate Cooper on how great the team was doing. I... I saw," I stutter over my words as I picture the gorgeous woman touching Coop with her lips pressed firmly to his.

"Take your time," Darlene says, handing me a tissue from the bedside table.

I take another deep breath, composing myself, then I just blurt it out like ripping off a bandage. "Cooper was kissing a woman."

"What?" she gasps, looking as shocked as I felt last night. Though, something tells me that she already knew this information. Especially since Coop called Colt last night looking for me. It only makes sense that he would tell them why I've come up missing in the first place.

"Yeah, he was kissing this beautiful woman. She looked like a supermodel pressed against him like only a lover would."

Another round of tears falls from my eyes and I soak them up with a tissue.

"Oh, honey, are you sure that's what really happened?"

"I know what I saw," I say defensively.

"I know that, but there has to be an explanation. I can't see Cooper being a cheater. He's too loyal for something like that. I mean, why would he have waited so long for you just to ruin it by kissing some other woman?"

"What do you mean he waited for me?" I ask, affronted.

"I mean exactly what I said. Coop has waited for you for years. Colt told me so," she adds.

"But why would he...? I don't understand," I say, feeling even more confused than ever.

"All I know is that he's been waiting for you to be ready or for some kind of sign that you wouldn't run for the hills when you found out about his daddy side."

I snort at that. Little did he know that all these years I've been daydreaming about him while reading dirty BDSM books about daddies and littles.

"That's just ridiculous," I say, shaking my head.

"Well, it's the truth," Darlene says. "That's why I can't see him doing anything to ruin what you have. You've both been so happy these last couple of weeks. It just seems so out of character for him."

She's not wrong about that. It does seem out of character. Now that I'm not focused solely on my hurt, I can see things a little more clearly. Maybe Darlene is right. Maybe things aren't as they seem. Is it possible that there's another explanation for what I saw?

The hurt part of my heart says, 'hell no,' the other part is hopeful. I want to squash the hopeful part because I feel like that's opening myself up for hurt. My mind replays her words over and over again.

He waited for me?

He's wanted me like I've wanted him all these years?

How is that possible?

I push aside those doubts. Those thoughts are the old Melinda. The old me would've scoffed at the idea that a man like Cooper would want me. A couple of weeks ago, I never would've believed it, but my confidence has grown after my time with him. Funny to think that considering how I'm feeling right now.

"What are you going to do?" she asks when I don't reply.

I shake my head. "Honestly, I'm not sure yet. I guess I need to talk to Cooper even though the thought terrifies me."

She wraps her arm around my shoulders and gives me a squeeze. "It'll work out one way or another."

I laugh sadly. "Yeah... I just don't know what the best way for it to work out is."

"All you can do is give Coop a chance to explain things, then go from there."

"What happens if I don't like what he has to say?" I ask, feeling another wave of sadness flow through my heart.

"Then you deal with it and keep moving forward."

Her words make perfect sense, but I don't like the connotation. I feel raw and a little bit broken.

Maybe more than a little broken. I'm not sure that it matters what Cooper has to say. I mean, I want to hear that it is all just a misunderstanding. That what I saw has been taken out of context, but I just don't know if that will help matters.

I never realized how much a broken heart would hurt. If it hurts this bad after just a couple weeks of being together, what will it feel like after months? Years? I can't imagine it. I don't think I could survive it.

"I guess the only thing left to do is talk to him," I say morosely.

"That's a girl!" Darlene says, sounding proud. She reaches over and hands me my phone. "I'll leave you to it."

I take the phone, holding it carefully like it's a ticking timebomb. She gives me a brief hug of encouragement, then leaves me alone with my cellphone and all kinds of doubts.

After a deep breath or three, I dial Coop. The second the phone rings, I nearly hang up. My courage waning. Before I can make the choice, Cooper's whiskey-smooth voice is on the line.

CHAPTER FOURTEEN

Cooper

I'M surprised when my phone rings and it's Mel... surprised and relieved. It's been twenty-four hours of silence. I've hated every second of it. I haven't slept or eaten since she disappeared on me. My stomach has been in knots, and my heart lodged in my throat. I can't imagine what she's been thinking about me, but none of it can be good.

"Mel," I say, letting every bit of my relief come through in those three little letters.

"Cooper," she says, sounding much more formal than I like.

"Where are you? I've been worried sick."

"I-I'm sorry I worried you," she says, sounding tearful. "I just needed space."

I let out a gusty sigh, running my hand down my face. "I understand. I'm so sorry for everything..."

I barely get the words out before Mel is interrupting me. "I don't want to do this over the phone. Can you come over?"

I'm both shocked and ecstatic that she wants me to come over. Though I don't like the tone of her voice. She sounds defeated, and I hate that.

"Of course."

"Can you meet me there in an hour?"

"I'll be there," I answer, not giving her a chance to change her mind.

"See you," she says just before hanging up.

I feel the loss of her voice like a gut punch. Part of me wants to rush over right now and not give her any more time to fill her mind with negative thoughts, but I won't do that. I'll give her the hour she asked for, even if the minutes drag by like torture.

AN HOUR LATER, I'm parked outside Mel's house, wiping sweat off my palms. I'm nervous for the first time in longer than I can remember. This could go really badly, and I can't even fathom surviving this going unfavorably. What happens if Mel doesn't believe me? Can we get over something like that? We've only been together a short time... is it enough for her to give me her trust?

The door opens before I even get out of my truck. Mel is waiting with her arms crossed over her middle like she's waiting for the first strike to come. My heart aches at the sight. I cross the distance between us in seconds, and without asking for permission, I pull her into my arms.

She sucks in a breath and stands stiff as a board in my arms. I run my hands over her back, trying to get her to relax into me, but she pulls away and takes two big steps back. I hate every inch of the distance she's putting between us. A millimeter of space would be too damn much.

"Babygirl..." I start but can't find the right words to express what I want to say. I've gone over it in my head a million times since she ran off, but now that she's in front of me, the words won't come. Seeing the hurt on her beautiful face and the defeat in her eyes has my heart aching for her. She's obviously spent the night going over all the possible scenarios, and none of them are good.

"Don't," she says, shaking her head. "Just don't."

Okay, she doesn't want me to call her babygirl. I can handle that even if I hate it.

"Mel... What you saw..."

"You, kissing another woman," she adds when I get stuck on my words again.

"I know it looked bad, but it's not what you think in the slightest. Yes, Janice kissed me, but it was one hundred percent unwanted."

She's still standing stiffly, her eyes narrowed as she looks at me suspiciously. "Who is Janice?"

"We dated a few times a couple years ago... it never went anywhere because she isn't who I had my heart set on."

That suspicious look doesn't leave her face as she considers my words. I understand the suspicion, but it still hurts.

"Why would she kiss you?"

I let out a rough sigh, running my hand through my hair, mussing it up further. "Janice isn't good with boundaries and doesn't like to hear no." I look at Mel with sincerity in my eyes, willing her to hear the truth of my words. "The only lips I want on mine are yours."

Mel sighs sadly, hugging herself. She looks fragile, and I desperately want to take her in my arms and make everything all right again. I know she's not there yet though.

"I believe you," she finally says, but it doesn't sound like a happy reunion is on the horizon. In fact, her words sound more like a break-up than a make-up and my heart clenches in my chest.

I move in close and reach out to cup her cheek, but she flinches back and shakes her head. "I need some time," she says, looking at me imploringly.

Her words say one thing, but her eyes are saying another. It gives me hope that things will be okay. I'm thanking God that she believes me, but at the same time, my heart is ripped to shreds that she won't let me close. I have to remind myself that it isn't what I want that matters, it's what she needs that's important, and right now, she's asking for space.

"Okay, love. I'll be right here waiting."

I step in close, pulling her into my arms before she has time to protest. Ever so slowly, she melts against me and hugs me back. I hate that this moment feels like a goodbye, but she's in my arms, and that's a good sign... Right?

I drop a kiss to the top of her head and leave, giving her the space she's asked for.

CHAPTER FIFTEEN

Melinda

THE SECOND MY DOOR CLOSES, I break down into tears. I know I sent him away, but I hate that he actually left. It's like he didn't even fight for me. Why is it so easy for him to walk away when it feels like the end of the world to me?

This sucks.

With a sad sniffle, I go and get the only comfort I have—chocolate chip cookie dough ice cream. I plop down on the sofa, make myself a burrito in my favorite throw blanket and open my ice cream. I settle in for a nice long mope.

Halfway through the pint of ice cream I decide that maybe I should get a cat because the love of an animal isn't nearly as painful as loving a person.

Wait. Love?

Do I love Cooper?

Crap. Yes, I think I do love him, and that scares

the pants off of me. If I didn't love him, I wouldn't already be a brokenhearted mess over this situation. How is it even possible that I fell for him so fast and hard? I have always been the cautious type, but it seems like I've thrown myself into the deep end and forgot how to swim.

I replay our conversation over and over in my head. Cooper was telling me the truth. I know he was, but I'm not sure if it matters at this point. My heart is broken, and we've only been together for a very short time. What would it be like if we continue for months or years and then something goes wrong?

I wouldn't survive it.

Setting my empty ice cream carton on the coffee table, I cover my head with the blanket and let the misery settle in because I can't risk it. I was fine being alone. This pain will pass, and I'll be back to where I was before I knew that Cooper returned my crush.

I spend the whole day in my blanket burrito. I give myself the day to mope and cry. Hopefully I can let out all the emotions this weekend before school restarts on Monday. The only time I get up is to move to my bed, where I promptly burrito up again and fall into a fitful sleep.

The night is full of dreams of Coop. If they were dreams about broken hearts, I might've been able to handle them better, but they aren't. No, my dreams are about all the amazing times we've shared.

In my dreams, Cooper spanks me and fucks me, and makes me scream his name. Over and over, he kisses me tenderly, holds me close, and has his wicked way with me. I wake up horny and sad.

I go through the motions of my normal Sunday routine. Though, I avoid going to the grocery store. I can't stand the thought of breaking down in the produce section. I'm still raw enough that it's a possibility.

My phone dings with a text from Darlene. *Hey girl, just checking in. How are you holding up?*

Do you want the truth or the candy-coated version? I ask.

I can imagine her shaking her head at me. *Truth, always.*

I'm miserable.

Tears fill my eyes again and I feel another crying jag coming on. I blink them back, trying to gain control of myself again. My phone rings. Darlene obviously isn't satisfied with texting now that she knows how I'm fairing.

"Hello," I murmur.

"Girl, tell me what happened. I thought you were going to talk to him yesterday and straighten everything out."

I sigh and sit down at my kitchen table where I

have my laundry piled up, waiting to be folded. "We did talk…"

"What did he say?"

"That it wasn't what it looked like, obviously."

"Do you not believe him?" she asks.

I cover my face with my hand and groan. "That's the problem. I do believe him."

"Uh… how is that a problem? Isn't it a good thing that you were mistaken about what happened?" she asks, clearly flummoxed.

"Yes… no… I don't know," I say, getting up from my chair and pacing around my kitchen. "I don't know how I feel about it. Yes, I'm glad that it was all a mistake and that it was the woman who kissed him and that he didn't engage in the kiss."

"So where does the no come in to play?" she asks.

I continue pacing, feeling like a caged tiger. "Because I don't know if it's worth it, Dar! Look at me. I'm a mess after just a couple weeks with him. What happens if we continue to date or whatever we are doing, and then things go wrong again?"

Darlene makes a clucking sound that tells me I'm about to get an earful. "Nothing worthwhile comes easily. Is trusting Cooper a risk? Yes, absolutely, but when things are good… it's totally worth the risks."

"How do you know?"

She laughs. "Look at Colt and me. Things weren't all roses for us at first either."

"Yeah, but you had a freakin' stalker who scared you into breaking things off with Colt. There's nothing like that happening here."

"Exactly. There is no reason for you not to be with Coop. Only your own fear is keeping you apart. The real question is if you're going to let fear of a broken heart override the possibility for happiness and love."

"I just don't know what to do. I need time to think..."

"Then take time to think. Just don't let your fears rule your decision."

"Thanks, girlie. I appreciate you talking me off the ledge."

"That's what friends are for," she says.

We say our goodbyes and I go back to my chores. I do my best to not think too hard about my situation. Yes, I asked for time to think, but I'm so raw right now that thinking is the last thing I want to do. Especially since Darlene's voice is running through my head, encouraging me to make the leap.

I am just finishing up the last load of laundry when my phone dings with a text. I pick it up, expecting it to be Darlene again, but it's Coop.

Hi babygirl. I hope you're okay. I miss you.

My heart constricts in my chest. I type out a quick I miss you too, then delete it just as quickly. I drop my phone on the sofa and decide I'll reply later... maybe.

I sleep like crap that night. It's Monday morning, and I feel like hot garbage water. I'm tempted to call in and spend the day hiding out, but I can't do that to my students. We have another competition coming up soon, and I won't disappoint them. They all work so hard, and I'm so proud of them. Even though it's going to be hard, I've got to pull on my big girl panties and go to work.

The car ride is spent on pep talks on what I will or won't do if I see Cooper. I will be polite and professional. I will not throw myself at him and beg him to take me back and forgive me for being scared. I will keep my tears on lockdown. I will not break down at school. I repeat these things like they are the most important affirmations ever.

My heart stops in my chest when I see Cooper standing beside his truck. It looks like he's waiting for me like he usually does, but surely he's not. Why would he wait for me when we aren't even together anymore?

I chew on my bottom lip, my nerves getting the better of me as I consider parking somewhere else... like on Jupiter. I take a deep breath and shore up my heart, then pull into my usual parking spot. I turn off the car and fuss around with my bags, stalling. I glance up at Cooper several times and feel a low beat of arousal building. It's impossible to be close to him and not feel attraction. He's wearing a white t-shirt with tight dark wash jeans. He looks like a wet dream walking. It's not until I get out of the car —finally—and notice the dark circles under his eyes and an overwhelming sadness that has taken over his usually happy demeanor.

He looks like I feel, which isn't good. At least I have makeup—something I rarely ever wear—to cover my own dark circles. I'm wearing it like warpaint because without it, I can't hide what's lingering underneath.

"Mel..." he says my name in that husky voice of his, and my stomach flip flops.

"Coop," I say with a nod, trying to hold back my emotions at being so close to him again.

My body wants to throw itself at him and melt into his warm chest. I want him to take away all my pain and make me happy again. I know he would in a heartbeat... but I have to make sure it's what I want before I put us both through a reunion like that.

He reaches out and takes my bags like he usually does. I let out a feeble protest, but he just gives me one of his stern looks, and I let go of the bags, letting him carry them for me. I realize this is his way of showing me that he's here for me even now when we are separated.

We walk together in silence, but I soak up the closeness. The scent of him. His masculine strength. Even when he's not touching me, I can feel it. He walks me to my classroom and sets my bags down. It looks like he's struggling just as hard as I am to keep his hands to himself. Seeing that makes me feel better about my own struggle.

"Have a good day, Mel," he says.

"You too, Coop."

I half expect him to kiss me like always, giving me a sneaky smooch before students start flooding into the room, but he doesn't. He simply turns on his heel and leaves the room. He doesn't even look back once.

I close my eyes tight and will myself to push down all the emotions I'm feeling. Now is not the time. After a few seconds, I find my center and fall into teacher mode. I'm not Cooper's brokenhearted babygirl anymore. I'm the badass band teacher who is going to lead her class to another state championship.

***

THE DAY DRAGS on and on. Having classes to distract me is good, but that raw ache in my chest is right there waiting to strike whenever I let my guard down even for a brief moment. I decide to eat lunch in my room, not feeling at all like being surrounded by people. I nibble on my sandwich but spend most of the time with my guitar. Over and over again, I try to lose myself in the music that usually flows through my veins as surely as blood does, but I can't seem to get there.

Music has always been my happy place, and now when I need it the most, it seems to have abandoned me. I'm so upset that I want nothing more than to throw my guitar across the room, but I carefully place the instrument back in its protective case, knowing I'd be mad at myself for destroying such a beautiful instrument.

The rest of the day moves a little faster. By the time the final bell rings, I'm ready to go back home and curl up on my couch. I'm emotionally drained and physically exhausted. I swear I've never been so tired in my life. I gather all of my things and head to the door. I stop abruptly, almost running smack dab into Coop's muscular chest.

"Sorry," I say, sounding breathless at just being in his presence, "I didn't see you there."

"It's okay, baby-" he cuts himself off before finishing the endearment I desperately want to hear from his lips. "Mel."

I chew on my bottom lip nervously. "Did you need something?" I ask when he doesn't say anything else. Not that I want the moment to end. Just being here with him makes me feel better than I have since Friday afternoon before things turned bad.

"I thought I would walk you to your car."

I blink up at him wondering why he's being so nice to me. He should be furious with me. Heck, I'm furious with myself and my own indecision. "You don't have to," I say as he takes my bags from my hands.

"I want to," he says simply.

"Okay." I smile softly at him, liking the fact that he's still showing me how much he cares and taking care of me even when we aren't together. My heart feels a little less conflicted knowing he's giving me time and space, but not too much space.

At my car, he opens the passenger door and sets down my things, then circles around and opens the driver's door for me. The wind ruffles my hair, and he automatically reaches out and tucks a loose strand behind my ear. I feel my cheeks heating in a blush at his touch. Especially when those fingers lightly graze over my jaw before falling away.

"So beautiful," he murmurs, looking deep into my eyes.

He's breaking down my resolve. Not that it's very strong to begin with. I need to get out of here before I give in to my desires.

"I should go..."

He closes his eyes, squeezing them tight like he's trying to hide his emotions before leveling that dark gaze on me. "Drive safe, babygirl," he says, not tripping over the endearment this time.

His voice and words flow over me in a protective

wave that pools in my belly in the form of desire. How I ever thought I could guard my heart against this man, I'll never know. Just this one casual experience is enough to prove that safeguarding my heart will be an uphill battle, one I'm not sure I want to travel.

CHAPTER SIXTEEN

Cooper

WATCHING MEL DRIVE AWAY SUCKS. Walking her to her car wasn't nearly enough time. Being so close to her was the highlight of my day, and the temptation to touch her was too much to resist. It might've only been the barest of brushes on her soft skin, but it was like a bottle of water magically appearing in the desert. It was exactly what I needed.

Once her car is out of sight, I debate on whether I should go home or head back inside to workout. It doesn't take me but a second to decide to workout. Going home now will just give me hours and hours of thinking about Mel, and I don't know that I could stop myself from calling her. Giving her space is the hardest thing I've ever done. I want nothing more than to force her into a conversation. To make her see what I do—that we are perfect for each other and that there is no reason for us to be apart... ever.

It's an easy choice to go workout. At least I'll be able to take out my frustrations on the weights and my body. I can lift until I can't anymore, then run on a treadmill until I'm unable to breathe. Hopefully with enough physical punishment, I'll be able to think about something other than my babygirl.

Ha. Not likely. It's still better than spending time twiddling my thumbs at home.

I'm almost to the safety of my gym when Darlene pops out of her classroom. "Hey, Coop!"

"Hi Darlene," I grumble, not feeling like chitchatting. The only person I want to talk to is on her way home with sad eyes and a broken heart that she won't let me heal.

"Are you going to the gym?"

"Yeah," I say suspiciously, wondering why she cares.

"Oh good! I'm glad Colt will have company in his workout. He missed it this morning," she giggles and blushes.

"Great, thanks for the heads up," I mumble.

Fuck me, I don't want to talk to Colt, and I know that's why he's working out in the afternoon. Yeah, he probably missed his morning workout because he was with Darlene this morning, but the fact that he stayed today isn't a coincidence.

"Have a good workout," she says cheerily.

I give her a nod and continue on my way to the gym. For a brief moment, I consider turning tail and running away. I really don't want to talk about anything, but at the same time, I know a good, punishing workout is exactly what I need.

I quickly change into my workout clothes and have barely gotten two steps into the weight room before Colt is racking his weights and sitting up on the bench to greet me. Though the almost hostile look on his face tells me that this conversation isn't going to be a friendly one.

"Colt," I say with a brief nod as I grab a set of dumbbells.

"So it's going to be like that then?" he growls. "You're just going to pretend everything is okay and that nothing's going on with you?"

I curl the dumbbell, giving him a withering look as I work my arms. "Not avoiding anything. I just don't see the point in hashing everything out."

"Bullshit," he says. "Darlene told me what Mel told her. I'd rather hear the story from you."

I drop the dumbbells to the ground in a loud thud. "What? You want to hear that Melinda saw Janice fucking Lin with her body pressed against me and her lips on mine? You want me to cry and tell you how Mel broke things off with me over it? You want to hear about how fucking mad I am?" I growl, feeling the anger crest to the boiling point.

"Yeah, I do."

"I'm pissed off, and I'll admit a little hurt that Mel doesn't trust me enough to know that I'd never do anything to hurt her. Especially cheat on her."

"Darlene says that Mel trusts your story about the kiss. She knows you didn't cheat."

I throw my arms up in the air and pace the room. "If she trusted me so damn much, why is she keeping us apart like this? Neither one of us are happy right now!"

"I think she's scared of being hurt. You know Mel hasn't been in a relationship before. This is all new to her. Throw in the kink factor and she's out of her depth."

Colt's words make sense. I know he's right, but I can't see past my own hurt right now. Not when I'm so worked up over everything. And especially not when I'm giving her space. I think that's my least favorite word in the dictionary—space.

Colt gets up and crosses the room to where I'm standing. He puts his hand on my shoulder and gives me an encouraging look. "Mel loves you; she just has to figure it out for herself. Don't give up on her." He pats my shoulder then walks off to the locker room, leaving me alone with my thoughts.

I work myself to the bone. Lifting and running. I don't stop until I'm drenched in sweat, and my riotous thoughts are back under control. Colt is right. Mel will figure things out, and we will have the rest of our lives to be together. I have to believe that this is just a bump in the road.

CHAPTER SEVENTEEN

Melinda

THE WEEK DRAGS on and on. Everyday Cooper waits for me to carry my bags both before school and after school. He hasn't texted or called once, and I'm not sure how I feel about that. I miss him. I miss us. I can't help wondering if he misses me as much as I do him or if I'm alone in my misery. His stubborn refusal to let me carry my own bags is the only thing that's keeping me from falling completely into a pit of despair.

"Good morning," Coop says as he opens my car door.

"Morning, Coop."

He gives me a strange look then reaches out to touch my cheek. He lightly runs his fingertips under my eyes where I know there are dark circles from lack of sleep.

"Are you okay?" he asks, looking genuinely concerned.

My eyes burn with unshed tears at his sweetness. He's the wronged party at this point. Yeah, there is the kiss with Janice, but it's my own stubbornness that's keeping us apart. I'm terrified of the feelings I have for him and even more terrified of what will happen if we get back together then fall apart again. I don't think I would survive it. I truly don't.

I shrug my shoulders, my words caught in my throat.

"You look exhausted," he growls lowly, sending a shockwave of lust through my system.

I shrug again. "I haven't been sleeping the best."

Anger flashes through his eyes briefly, then is gone as quick as it appeared. "Babygirl, you need to take care of yourself."

I look at my toes at his reprimand. Does he think I'm not sleeping on purpose? I can't sleep because my dreams are inundated with him. Everything from sexy dreams of our times together to nightmares about him disappearing. I spend hours a night either turned on or chasing after him in my dreams. Neither are good for productive sleep.

"I'm trying," I have to bite back the desire to call him daddy. God, I want to so bad.

His shoulders slump, and a sad look crosses his face. "I know, babygirl. I hate seeing you like this."

I sniffle. "I hate feeling like this."

"Let me take you to dinner tonight. We should talk..." he says, looking at me with hopeful eyes.

I don't even have to think about my answer. I've pushed him away, and it's obviously not working. Time to try something else. "Okay. Dinner."

He smiles widely, and there is a spark in his eyes for the first time in days. My heart feels lighter at the sight. Just that look on his face is enough for me to be glad that we are going to talk, even if I don't know what my decision is yet. I'm obviously not doing a good job at deciding for myself. Maybe talking to him will help.

He walks me to my classroom, and before I can protest, he brushes his lips over my cheek. "Have a good day."

My cheeks turn a bright shade of pink. "You too," I manage through my shyness. I feel like I'm right back to where I started. I've reverted back to the shy, blushing virgin that I was before we started dating.

The day is a frustrating one. My students won't quit screwing around. Everyone seems to have a case of the Fridays. They don't want to work, and I can hardly blame them. The more I think about Coop and our dinner date, the more I want this day to be over with.

Finally, the last bell rings, and school is over. The students stream out of my classroom, and I quickly gather my things, ready to get the heck out of here too. Excitement at seeing Coop and knowing that I'll be spending real time with him has me smiling a genuine smile for the first time in days. Like always, Coop is waiting for me outside my classroom. He greets me with a smile and reaches for my bags. I don't grumble about him taking them. Instead I hand them over happily.

It feels great to smile. I feel lighter and happier. Nothing has changed, not really, but knowing that we are going to spend some time together has me practically giddy.

"How was your day?" he asks.

"Long," I say with a shy smile. "How was yours?"

"Long." He smirks. "I had something more pressing than yelling at a bunch of teenaged boys waiting for me."

I blush, knowing that he's talking about me. I can't get over how happy that makes me. I file this feeling away for later, knowing that it will play a huge part in how our upcoming conversation is going to play out.

"I made a reservation at Teddy's. Would you like to ride together?" he asks, looking vulnerable for once like he's expecting to be let down.

Part of me thinks that riding together is a bad idea. I'm still not positive how things will play out with our talk, though my heart is definitely tugging me in one direction. If we ride together, then there is no escaping. I'll be stuck if things go badly. I chew on my bottom lip, considering my options.

Common sense flies right out the window at his down-trodden look. He really does think I'm going to turn him down. I mentally shake myself. Regardless of how this dinner ends, Coop and I will always be friends. We may not be romantically involved when this night is over, but we will remain friends. At least I hope we can be. I can't see a life for myself without him in it in some way.

"Together," I say with a smile.

His answering smile makes my heart sing. We stow my work things in my car, then like the gentleman he is, Coop helps me up into his truck.

"Thanks," I say shyly.

"What have I said about thanking me?" he teases, smirking at me knowingly.

"I guess you'll have to keep reminding me."

"I can do that," he says with a charming smile. The one that makes my stomach break out with butterflies and my core to clench. Crazy how just a simple smile can have such a visceral reaction from me.

The drive to the restaurant is quiet but not uncomfortable. It's like we've both decided not to discuss anything until we arrive. The comfortable silence between us makes me miss our quiet moments together. It fills me with longing.

He pulls up to the club and drives around back

to the restaurant entrance. I laugh to myself that I ever considered the club as a children's playground. I'll never forget the look on Cooper's face when he told me exactly what the club was and the hungry way his eyes bore into mine.

"I hope you don't mind coming here. I don't want to give you the wrong idea," he says.

I smile reassuringly and bravely reach across the truck to put my hand on his thigh.

"It's perfect. We will be able to talk more freely here than anywhere else." And that's one hundred percent true. The Playground is a judgment-free zone, and so is the attached restaurant.

I'm a little surprised when we are seated in a private dining room. Cooper didn't just get a standard reservation. He reserved one of the individual dining rooms where we will be completely alone and able to talk without any nosy, listening ears. I'm grateful for his thoughtfulness. Just because this is a judgment-free zone, I still don't like the idea of anyone listening in to what we are going to discuss.

The fate of our relationship—and my heart—are on the line with this conversation. It's the most important talk of my life.

We are seated and the hostess leaves us with our menus and the promise that our waiter will be with us shortly. I nervously look at the menu, knowing that with how nervous I am, I won't be able to stomach a single bite, let alone decide on what to eat. I'm looking over the options for the third time when Coop grabs my menu and sets it aside.

"Let me help."

I remember all the times he's ordered for me and how perfect his selections have been. My building anxiety suddenly lessens as a wave of gratitude flows through me. "Thanks, da-" I barely catch myself from calling him daddy... we aren't there yet. "Thanks."

He gives me a sad look, and I know it's because he wants to hear me calling him daddy again. He wants our relationship back to what it was, and despite my fears, I'm figuring out that I want it too.

The waiter comes in, and Cooper places our order, getting me grilled chicken with five cheese macaroni on the side. Perfect as always. When the waiter leaves, Coop reaches across the table and holds my hand. It's only then that I realize I was thrumming my fingers on the tabletop, probably driving him crazy.

"Sorry," I say with a blush.

"No need to apologize. You're nervous. It's understandable."

"This just feels..." I pause, not knowing how to put it into words. "Huge," I add lamely.

He gives me a warm smile. "It does. It's going to be okay; you know that, right?"

I shake my head because no, I really don't know that. And that right there is the crux of the issue. I don't know how things are going to end with us, and that's what has me freaking out.

"No matter what is decided here, everything will be okay," he reassures me.

"I'm just scared," I admit.

"I know you are, darlin'. I would be willing to give up my man card and admit to being scared too if it would help you."

I smile at that because, yeah, it does help.

"I know I've already apologized, but I feel like I need to tell you how sorry I am again. I want to make sure you know that I would never willingly hurt you like that. Never."

My heart pounds in my chest because this is the moment. This is where I either tell him we are good and move forward with our relationship, or I break it off. This moment will change both of our futures, and it feels huge. Because it is huge, I realize.

"I know you wouldn't, Cooper. You're a good man. I'm sorry that I didn't give you a chance to explain things that night. I was just so... shocked and hurt that I couldn't see past my feelings to the reality of the situation."

"Babygirl," he says, squeezing my fingers in his strong hand. "You have nothing to apologize for. None of this is your fault."

I squeeze his fingers back. Despite his words, I'm not reassured because this last week of misery is my fault. My fear is keeping us from being together.

"What can I do to make this better for you?" he asks.

God, could this man be any more perfect? I'm the one keeping us apart, yet he is the one trying to make me feel better about it. I'm the cause of our continued heartache, and he's trying to fix it even if it means we won't end up together in the end.

"I'm scared."

"I know, babygirl. I don't know what to say that would make you any less afraid."

"Guarantee that we will always be together and happy?" I say with a hopeful expression.

He chuckles. "Relationships just don't work like that, but I can guarantee I will do everything in my power to make sure you're happy and that your heart is safeguarded."

I let out a little sigh. "I know you will. I've been miserable without you... daddy."

The smile he gives me is megawatt it's so happy. I've never seen him so happy. He stands from his chair and circles around to my side of the table, and falls to his knees beside me, then I'm tugged into his arms. I snuggle against him, feeling like everything is right in my world once again.

Our lips meet, and we kiss slow and sweet in reunion. The kiss quickly deepens, turning heated. The waiter picks that moment to show up with our food, but Coop doesn't let me go, he just continues holding me, and I continue holding him. The waiter quickly sets our dishes on the table then excuses himself quietly.

As soon as he's gone, Cooper's lips are back on me, kissing my cheek, my jaw, my neck, back up to my lips... his mouth is everywhere, teasing me with gentle swipes of his lips. It feels so good, so right. I let out a happy little moan as he nips my earlobe. My fingers thread into his hair, holding him to me as he kisses me.

Our tongues dance and stroke, slicking against each other hotly. I shift on the chair feeling turned on and antsy. He winds his fingers through my hair, tugging my head back, controlling the kiss like the dominant man he is. My pussy clenches at the small bite of pain. I moan into his lips, encouraging him.

His other arm wraps around my waist, and he tugs me from the chair until I'm straddling him. I groan when I feel the hard ridge of his cock beneath his pants. Oh, Jesus, he feels good against me like this. I wrap my legs around his waist, wriggling my pussy over the top of his hard cock.

With one hand in my hair and one on my bottom, he controls me completely. He holds my head exactly where he wants it so he can deepen our kisses while his other hand helps me writhe on top of him until I'm panting and close to orgasm.

We kiss like that for endless moments, me riding the edge of release while he teases and torments me. We completely lose ourselves, kissing our reunion. I can feel his heart pounding in his chest below my palms, racing like my own. Before I can reach my pleasure, Coop breaks away from my lips. I look at him with lust-glazed eyes as I wantonly rub against him. It's only been a week apart, but it feels like it's been a lifetime since he's touched me. I'm a livewire waiting to spark into flames.

"Fuck, babygirl. You're killing me here," he groans, gripping my ass tight in his palms.

I blink innocently at him, wriggling my bottom. "Don't know what you're talking about," I gasp.

"Like hell you don't. Rubbing this hot little pussy all over me like you're starving for my cock."

"I'm completely famished, daddy," I moan as I rock on him enticingly.

"I'm not fucking you on the floor," he growls lowly, stopping my movements with his firm grip.

I whimper, hating that he's preventing me from taking what I want from him.

"It's private," I say pleadingly. Now that I've decided to be brave and hand over my heart, I seem to have found that bold streak he brings out in me again.

"Yes, it is, but I'm still not fucking you here on the floor like an animal."

"There's a wall you could use instead." I smirk and trail my hands down his chest toward his waistband.

"Fuck, you're tempting me, kitten. But not here.

When I take you again, it'll be at home in a bed, just you and me."

I pout at him but secretly love that. I love that he knows exactly what he wants, and it's not a quick fuck. He wants to take his time with me. Deep down, I want that too. I'm just impatient to get it.

"Well, what are we waiting for?" I ask boldly.

He squeezes my ass in a punishing grip. "Someone has found her sassy side awful quick."

I shrug. "I just know what I want and don't want to wait for it anymore."

Coop's lips tip up in a knowing grin sending my heart aflutter. "Let's get out of here then."

THE CAR RIDE TO Coop's place is quick and filled with sexual tension. He holds my hand the whole way, threading his fingers through mine and teasing me with gentle caresses of his thumb along my wrist. Who knew such an innocent touch could be such a freakin' turn-on?

By the time we arrive, I'm wetter than I've ever been and ready to crawl into his lap right here in the truck. The only thing keeping me in my seat is the fervent way he said the next time he takes me, will be in a bed. I won't begrudge him that. Besides, beds mean all kinds of possibilities, and I want them all.

I stay in my seat as he circles around the truck to my door. He opens the door and tugs me out, kissing me fiercely before my feet even fully hit the ground. The kiss ends just as quickly as it started. I've hardly had a chance to catch my breath when he bends and lifts me up over his shoulder. I gasp and giggle as his hand finds my bottom in a playful spank. He uses his grip on my ass to hold me in place as he quickly strides into the house. He doesn't put me down until he's tossing me onto his bed.

The look on Coop's face is positively feral. I lick my lips, turned on beyond belief by the possessive look in his eyes. He looks like he's barely holding on to his control... I want him to let loose. I want him to completely lose that firm control he holds on to.

I let out a squeal when he grabs my ankles and tugs me to the edge of the bed, my skirt riding up until my panties are on display. He falls to his knees between my spread thighs, throwing my legs over his shoulders.

"Tsk, tsk... look how wet you are for me, naughty girl."

I moan lowly when he teases his fingertips over my damp panties. "I can't help it. I want you too much."

"What do you want?" he asks, running his rough palms up and down my thighs coming closer and closer to my core with every upward motion until his fingers are teasing at the edge of my panties.

"You, daddy. All of you."

He lets out a low growl in appreciation of my words. "Do you want my fingers?" he asks, teasing along my panty line.

"Yes," I gasp.

"What about my mouth on this sweet cunt?"

"God, yes..."

"Hmm..." he murmurs, lightly petting over the gusset of my panties, teasing me. "And my thick cock? Do you want that buried deep? Fucking you?"

"Please," I beg, wanting it all. I'm greedy for it. I want everything he has to offer. I'm walking the edge of sanity, ready to plunge to the other side if he doesn't touch me soon.

"I'm not sure, babygirl. You've been awful naughty, keeping me away from what's mine."

His fingers dip below my panties, pulling a cry from my lips as he gently caresses my wet folds. It's not enough to bring me to release, just a gentle tease that is meant to drive my arousal higher. His fingers move slickly along my pussy, teasing up around my clit, then back down until he's rimming my ass. I whimper and squirm away from the forbidden touch. He lays his arm over my lower stomach, pinning me in place so he can touch me wherever he wishes.

"Maybe I should punish this sexy ass of yours,"

he growls. His fingers circle my bottom hole, pulling a gasp and moan as he gently applies pressure. From his touch, I don't think he means a spanking. My heart skips a beat, and my core clenches at the dirty threat.

"I've never..." I say stupidly. Of course I've never. Until a short time ago, I was a virgin in all ways.

"I know," he says, looking darkly into my eyes. His lustful gaze is enough to have me relaxing into his touch. I can see he's in control yet totally aroused by the possibility of taking my ass. I trust him with this. I trust him with everything.

He leans in and laps at my clit with his tongue, growling in frustration when my panties get in his way. I gasp in shock when he rips them from my body. The lace falling away like tissue paper. "Cooper!"

He gives me a satisfied smirk. "Oops." I let out a breathy giggle at his playfulness. Even when he's in full dom mode, he's still my loving daddy. "Hope you weren't attached to those."

I shake my head because he could rip a dozen pairs of my finest panties if it meant that he'd lick my clit again. "Good," he growls, lowering his mouth to my pussy and sliding his tongue from my aching hole up to my clit.

"Daddyyy..." I squeal when he licks me over and over, driving me up and up until I feel like I'll combust at the slightest touch to my clit. The frustrating man just teases circles around my clit though. Never touching me in the way I need to push me over the edge. "Please," I beg.

One small swipe of his tongue. One touch of his fingers. Hell, one breath on my clit, and I'll explode into a million pieces.

"Not yet," he chides. "You'll come when I say."

I let out a keening moan sounding like a wounded animal, but I nod my acceptance. "Yes, daddy. I'll be your good girl."

He gives me a mischievous smile. "There was never any doubt."

I cry out when he flips me over without a warning until I'm draped over the edge of the bed, my ass in the air, my toes barely touching the ground to help me keep my balance. I clutch at the covers, knowing what's coming. I don't even have time to prepare before his hand cracks down on my ass in two quick spanks.

"Do you know why you're getting this spanking?"

"Yes, daddy. I was a bad girl," I gasp through the pain of another spank.

"You didn't trust me. You didn't trust in us," he scolds.

Tears fill my eyes, but not from the spanking that he's slowly and precisely administering. "I'm sorry. I was so scared..."

"I know you were, babygirl. I forgive you."

The words are a balm to my soul. I let go of all of the guilt I've been secretly harboring, hiding it even from myself. He's right that I didn't trust him, which seems ridiculous now. Our relationship is built on a foundation of trust. I could never give myself over like this to a man I don't trust implicitly. I relax into the bed, accepting my punishment.

His hand falls again and again, creating a stinging heat in my skin. He's not spanking me hard, just enough to warm my skin and cause my pussy to tingle and grow wetter. He pauses in his punishment to push his fingers between my legs. He slides wetly into my pussy, pumping his fingers deep twice before pulling them out and up to my tight bottom hole. I gasp when he circles my back entrance.

"One day, I'm going to take this tight little ass of yours and you're going to beg me for it," he promises.

I whimper into the sheets, fisting them in my hands as he teases me with his touch and words. I'm ready to beg him to do it now; it feels so good. So naughty. I press back into his fingers, silently letting him know I want more. He doesn't disappoint. He applies slight pressure to that sensitive ring of muscles, teasing the tip of one finger into my ass. I nearly come undone when his other hand teases down to play with my clit.

"Oh, God. Daddy!" I cry out. "I'm going to come."

He lets out a feral growl, leaning over my body until his lips are by my ear, his hands still working their magic. "Do it, babygirl. Come all over my fingers."

He pushes his finger further into my ass then pinches my clit. I explode. My muscles clench down as he thrusts his finger in and out of me, his fingers rubbing tight circles around my clit, pushing me higher and higher as I wail out my pleasure. I come so hard I see stars and tears fill my eyes. I've never come so hard in all of my life.

He slowly pulls his finger from my bottom and gives one gentle tap to my clit that sends a shudder through my body as I have another mini orgasm from the almost too rough touch to my sensitive clit. Before I have a chance to catch my breath, Cooper flips me over and crawls between my legs, pushing me up the mattress until I'm in the center of the bed.

I'm not sure when, but at some point he stripped his clothes and is hovering over me in all his naked glory. I'm still fully dressed, minus my panties which he destroyed in his eagerness. I expect him to strip me so we are equally naked, but he doesn't make a move to. Instead, he notches his cock to my entrance and sinks into me. My pussy clenches around him, still sensitive from my orgasm.

"Fuck, you're so goddamn tight."

I don't know if it's that I'm so tight or if it's just

that he's so damn big because he stretches me in the most perfect way. His thick, hard length sinks into me to the hilt and I can't hold back my moans of pleasure. I don't even try to silence them. He grinds himself into me, rubbing against my oversensitive clit as he does.

"Oh, God..."

"Not God... just your daddy."

"Yessss..." I hiss, clenching around him. I love the naughtiness of calling him my daddy. I love that little nod to the taboo. Others might not understand the appeal but fuck them. He's my daddy, and I'm his babygirl, and we are perfect.

He slowly pulls out until just the head of his big cock is poised at my entrance. I whine in anticipation, wondering if he's going to go fast or slow. Will he tease us both, or will he bring us to quick releases? My question is answered when he pushes back inside me with slow precision, setting a maddening pace that has my pleasure building slow but steady.

My arms encircle his neck as he leans down to kiss me. I run my fingers through his hair, holding him to me as his lips lightly caress mine in light, teasing kisses. He nips my bottom lip, and I open for him. His tongue slides against mine in the sweetest kiss I've ever had. He's making sweet love to my mouth just like he is to my pussy. Tears well up in my eyes at the exquisite pleasure of it.

Coop grips my ass in one big palm, canting my hips until with every stroke of his thick length he's rubbing against my g-spot.

"Ohmygod, daddy," I moan. "Right there..."

He lightly nips my lip, then kisses a line down my jaw to my ear. "That's it, babygirl. Let daddy take care of you."

I nod, gripping his shoulders as he kisses down my neck. He lets out a growl of frustration when he gets to my shirt. I move to unbutton my blouse, but he knocks my hands aside and grips it on both sides, giving me a questioning look. I nod my head, and in the next second, the buttons go flying as he rips my shirt open.

Fuck, that was hot. My nipples pebble under my bra, and my pussy clenches down on his thrusting cock. His fingers deftly release the front clasp of my bra, and then his mouth is on me. Licking and nipping at my hard nipples, never stopping his thrusting hips. He plays with my nipples. Each swipe of his tongue and nip of his teeth sends a line of pleasure to my clit like the two are connected by some invisible cord.

It's all too much. I'm going to come again and there's no stopping it. It builds and builds until it feels too big for my body. I thrash my head back and forth and grip his hips with my legs, trying to stop the build-up. It's too big. It feels like I'll fall into a million pieces that will never be put back together again if he doesn't stop.

"I can't. Daddy... please..."

"You can," he growls against my breast before biting down on the pale skin. That one harsh touch throws me over the precipice.

My body jolts up as my pussy clenches down on his cock. His thrusts turn harder, faster, drawing out my release. Bringing me to a higher ledge. Forcing me up and up until it's almost celestial. My nails dig into his back, and my teeth sink into the hard muscle of his shoulder as I try to ground myself. It does no good because that thick hard cock just keeps pounding into me. Driving me over that edge again.

I scream to the heavens until my voice is hoarse and I'm out of breath. Fireworks explode throughout my body. My eyes are blind to the room from the sheer magnitude of the explosion that's wracking my body. I'm barely cognizant of Cooper reaching his own release. Some distant part of me registers his groan and the warm heat of him filling me with his come.

I collapse back to the mattress, my body completely limp and my mind practically dead to the world. My lungs suck in oxygen like they've been deprived for hours. I finally blink my eyes open and find the face of the man I love looking down on me with a satisfied smile and warmth in his eyes.

"I love you, Melinda."

I swallow thickly. This is a huge moment. Cooper just told me he loves me. I don't know what to say. I mean... I love him. I do... God, I love this man with all of my heart. But can I find the courage to say it?

I lick my lips and his eyes trail down to them. He leans in and kisses me gently. "You don't have to say anything," he murmurs, kissing me again, this time deeper causing my toes to curl.

I thread my fingers through his hair and return the achingly sweet kiss. When he lingers at my lips, kissing me like I'm the world's most precious thing, I make my decision. Why would I hold back from telling the man I love that I love him too?

Yes, it's fast. Probably too fast for most, but it's not too fast for us. We've already overcome so much in our short relationship, and we've come out the other side stronger and closer than ever.

I break our kiss and look him in the eyes. Wanting him to see the truth of my words. "I love you, too, Cooper. So much."

His smile is so bright it's blinding. His lips crash to mine in a searing hot kiss. I gasp and wriggle against him when I feel his cock thicken against me again.

He lets out a low growl. "Again? My girl is needy today."

"Again," I moan.

He laughs, rolling us until I'm straddling him. His hard cock is trapped between our bodies, pressing against my clit in the most delicious way. I rock against him, shivering at the sensation because I'm still so sensitive.

Coop's big hands grip my hips, and I reach between us, lining his cock up with my opening before sinking down on him slowly. He's so big this way. He goes so deep it hurts so good. My pussy flutters around him as I let myself adjust to this new position. His grip on my hips tightens, but he leaves me in charge of my movements. I rock on top of him causing us both to moan. I slowly raise my hips then let my own weight draw me back down on him.

"Ohhh..." I gasp.

"That's it, baby. Take your pleasure."

I do it again and again, loving the feel of him so deep inside me. My hands roam up my body, teasing my nipples as I ride his thick cock. He slaps my hands away, replacing them with his own. He tugs and pinches my nipples much harder than I ever would. Each little pain is like a shockwave through my body pushing my desire that much higher.

This time when I start my downward slide, he lifts his hips meeting me. I cry out at the intense sensation.

"Like that?" he asks knowingly.

I nod my head, raising up again and falling until

we crash together again. Over and over, we move setting an almost punishing rhythm. I fall to his chest, unable to keep my balance as his thrusts become harder, more purposeful. Our breaths mingle as our lips touch in an almost kiss as he fucks me from below, holding me in place so that he's now in charge. I willingly give it up to him, loving every bit of what he's doing.

"Fuck. I'm going to come. Going to fill this tight little pussy with my come."

I groan at his dirty words. I love his dirty talk. It turns me on like crazy and is enough to push me off the ledge into another earthquaking orgasm. My pussy clenches down and his cock jerks inside me as we come together. Our movements slow until I'm collapsed over his chest, his cock still twitching inside me as he pours the last of his release inside me.

I shiver when he strokes my back, petting my skin as I come down from the high of another powerful release. My eyes fall closed and I doze cuddled in his safe embrace.

CHAPTER EIGHTEEN

Cooper

I WRAP Mel up in my arms, loving the feel of her gentle weight against me. She dozes in my arms while I happily hold her close. I'm so glad that she's forgiven me and is where she belongs—with me. I've never been so happy as the moment she said, 'I love you.' She bravely gave me a second chance—gave us a second chance.

I honestly don't know how I could've gone on without her. Just a week apart and my world was dark and dreary. I need her too damn much. I press a kiss to the top of her head and feel her smile against my chest.

"Welcome back, babygirl," I murmur.

She giggles breathlessly. "I think you killed me there for a minute."

"What a way to go though."

"Mmm..." she murmurs, snuggling in closer.

"Let's get cleaned up before you pass out on me," I say.

"Or we could just lay here forever..."

"Nope, shower first, then snuggles," I say, giving her bottom a firm pat.

Mel groans her displeasure. "Do we have to? I'm comfy."

I roll us until she's underneath me and I'm fitted between her legs again. I lean in and kiss her deeply. She instantly responds, kissing me passionately. Our tongues slick together in a dance as old as time. I gently cup her face in my hands, turning the kiss slow and sweet. Mel's arms wrap around me, holding me to her. We are connected in the most basic of ways. It feels like our hearts are one in this moment.

My cock hardens between us and she gasps. I slowly slide inside her, making love to her in a slow, steady pace. The lust that was guiding us before has smoldered down into something softer, sweeter. Our lips never part as I thrust into her. She wraps her legs around me, her hips moving at my pace.

She gasps and moans into my lips while her pussy clenches down on me. Her orgasm is coming on fast, and I'm not going to be far behind her. She pulls away from my lips and looks at me with love in those blue-gray eyes of hers. Her hand cups my cheek as she tells me how much she loves me.

Her lips part in a moan as her eyes fall closed for a moment before popping open again like she doesn't want to miss a moment of this. I lean in and nuzzle against her, kissing her gently.

"I'm going to come," she gasps. "Oh God, Cooper..."

"Come, babygirl."

And she does with a breathless moan and the words 'I love you' falling from her lips again.

"I love you, too," I groan as I'm overcome with my own release.

We lay connected, both breathless. I nuzzle against her nose to nose, then press kisses to both her cheeks, her eyelids, her forehead... I kiss her everywhere in thanks for being my girl. Showing her how much I care with every little peck of my lips.

"How is it always so wonderful?" she asks.

"It's because it's us, kitten. We're perfect together."

She smiles brightly at me and hugs me close. "We really are."

"Now, let's get cleaned up. I need to feed my girl."

"But it's so nice here like this," she says, hugging me tight. Her stomach picks that moment to rumble, proving my point. Her cheeks turn pink from embarrassment. "Maybe I'm a little hungry."

I pull her up from the bed and lead her to the bathroom. We take a quick shower then head into the kitchen to see what I can pull together for dinner. I end up making salmon and steamed veggies, nothing fancy.

"It's definitely not as good as Teddy's."

"It's perfect," she says with a smile.

After we eat, we crawl back into bed. Mel lets out a little sigh of contentment as she snuggles in against me. I kiss the top of her head and run my fingertips up and down her back, soothing her.

"Mmm... that feels good."

I smirk, recognizing the neediness in her tone, but knowing she's worn out. "Sleep, sweet girl."

Within minutes she's softly snoring against my chest. It's adorable and makes my heart sing at the trusting way she falls asleep in my arms. Shortly after, I fall asleep too.

I WAKE up alone in bed and grumpy at my girl not being in my arms still. I pull on a pair of sweatpants and go in search of my love. I find her in the kitchen dancing around in one of my t-shirts while she cooks something on the stove. I don't even try to hold back my smile at the sight of her so carefree and happy in my home. I could wake up to her every day and never get tired of it.

I take a seat at the breakfast bar and watch her as she moves around my kitchen, completely oblivious to being watched. She shakes her ass to whatever song she's got in her head and my cock twitches in my pants at the sight. I let out a soundless groan when she reaches into the upper cupboard to retrieve plates. My shirt lifts showing the lower curves of her butt cheeks, giving me a peek at what's mine.

She turns and jumps at seeing me sitting here.

"Oh my God! You scared me," she blurts.

"Sorry, kitten. I was just enjoying the view."

Her cheeks turn a fetching shade of pink. "I made breakfast. I was going to bring it to you in bed." Her lips turn down in a pout like she's upset that I ruined her plans.

I stalk across the room to her and pull her against my chest. "You didn't have to do that, babygirl."

Her arms wrap around me, and she rests her head over my heart. "I know, I wanted to. It's just pancakes."

With a finger under her chin, I tip her face up to mine and kiss her gently. Just that gentle touch of lips is enough to have my cock hard in my pants. I run my hand down her back until I'm cupping one bare butt cheek, pulling her against me so she can feel my hard length. She lets out a little moan of appreciation and wiggles against me, letting me know she's ready and willing.

I deepen the kiss, tangling my tongue with hers hungrily. She easily submits to my ministrations, dancing her tongue along with mine until we are both breathless. Somehow I manage to gain a modicum of control and pull away from her sexy body.

"Breakfast," I growl, gripping her ass again.

She gives me a hungry look, but I know it's not pancakes she wants. Too bad, my babygirl made pancakes, and I'm eating them... then I'm eating her for dessert.

"I don't want the weekend to be over," Mel sighs as she towel dries her hair.

I pull her closer against my side and kiss the top of her head. "Just because the weekend is over doesn't mean anything is changing."

"I know that. I just hate that our little bubble is being popped by reality."

I let out a low growl because, as far as I'm concerned, this weekend is our new reality. Her and I spending every moment together. That's all that I want from now until forever. I just need to convince her of that. I cross the room, closing the distance between us. Using the front of her robe, I pull her into me. Cupping her cheek, I make sure she's looking at me so she will see the seriousness of my words.

"This is our new reality, babygirl. You and me, there's nothing else."

She gives me a bright smile and leans up to kiss me, balancing on tiptoe. "I love you, Cooper Crane."

"And I love you, Melinda Young."

She lets out a little giggle and goes back to getting ready for work. I'm already dressed and ready so I head to the kitchen to fix coffee for my girl. Twenty minutes later, she comes bustling out of her room dressed in a knee-length skirt with a shirt that fits her like a second skin. I've never seen her dress this way for work before, and I grin knowing that she's dressing this way because she's starting to feel more confident in herself.

"You look amazing, kitten," I say, kissing her lips tenderly.

"Thanks, daddy," she says with a blush.

I hand her a cup of coffee and she gives me a thankful smile before taking a sip. "Mmm... perfect, thanks."

"You're welcome. I wouldn't dare let you out in public without a little caffeine in your system," I tease. "The students wouldn't survive it."

She laughs. "I'm a perfect ray of sunshine without caffeine, thankyouverymuch."

It's my turn to laugh because she is definitely grumpy without that first cup of coffee. Something I learned the first night she slept over at my place. I'm not a coffee drinker and I thought she would cry when she learned that I don't have a coffee pot. Something I rectified right away. I'll always do whatever it takes to make my girl happy.

She quickly downs her coffee, then rinses out her mug.

"Ready?" I ask.

Mel gives me a little pout. "Would it change anything if I said no?"

I throw back my head and laugh, then pull her into my arms. "No, it won't change anything, but it will get you a kiss."

"Then, no. No, I'm not at all ready."

She tips her head back and closes her eyes, ready for the promised kiss. I dare not disappoint her, pressing my lips to hers in a heated kiss. I pull away and she lets out a little kitten-like growl, then tugs me back into her lips for another kiss. A kiss that quickly gets out of control when her hands wander down my chest to the front of my pants. She rubs her hand against my cock, making me hard. I grip her wrist and pull her hand away.

"Naughty girl."

She gives me a sultry look, not in the least bit repentant. "Always for you," she smirks.

"Going to work with a hard-on isn't exactly at the top of my list of things to do today."

She shrugs. "It's only fair considering my panties are going to be wet all day thinking about you."

I growl and tug her against me for another kiss.

This time it's my hands that are trailing over her, dipping down and raising her skirt until my fingers slide under her panties. She's already wet and ready for me just like she said. I look at the clock and see that we have a few minutes... definitely not long enough to do all the things I want to do with her, but long enough to give us both what we need.

I quickly turn her, pushing her front against the counter. I pin her there with my big body, grinding my cock against her ass. "Is this what you wanted? A dirty fuck before school like a bad girl?"

"Yes, daddy!" she cries out, pressing back against my cock.

I tug her skirt up above her ass and pull her panties aside as I free my cock from my pants. I slick my fingers through her lips, making sure she's good and soaked for me. "Dirty, dirty girl, all horny and wet for me."

"Always," she moans, thrusting her ass back into my touch.

Without preamble, I line my cock up with her entrance and thrust inside her wet heat.

"Fuck, babygirl. You're so fucking tight."

She gasps and moans as I ride her hard. Fucking into her tight sheath, making it so she'll feel me long after I'm done.

"Harder," she moans. "Fuck me, daddy."

With a punishing grip on her hips, I do as she says and fuck her like a man possessed. And I am possessed. Possessed by this little girl who has stolen my heart and soul. I reach around and pinch her nipple over her clothes, playing with the tight bud like it's my new favorite toy. Mel squeals at the sharp pain, but her hips press back into me telling me she loves how I'm owning her body.

Her pussy clenches down hard, the sounds of our sex fill the room around us. She's so wet that I glide in and out without any resistance. Every stroke leading us both to completion. I release her nipple and encircle her throat in my hand, leaning over her body until my lips are poised at her ear.

"Come for me, kitten."

She gasps and lets out a low moan as her pussy clamps down on my aching cock. She shudders and shakes, her orgasm washing over her on a sharp cry of my name.

"That's a good girl," I growl. "Gonna come deep inside this little pussy. Leave you messy all day."

She groans at my dirty words. "Yes, daddy. Fill me up... please." She begs so prettily for my come, and there's no holding back anymore. My balls draw up and my cock throbs inside of her, emptying my come deep inside her just like I promised.

Mel collapses to the countertop, her knees giving way until the only thing holding her up is my firm grip on her hips. I drop a tender kiss to the back of her neck, slowly pulling my cock from her snug pussy. A pearly white trail of my release trickles from her and I groan at the sight. I pull her panties back into place and give her pussy a pat.

She shivers at the tease.

"Sensitive?" I ask.

"Very," she giggles.

I help her stand and fix her clothes. Her face is flushed, and her eyes are bright. She looks well-fucked. I pull her in for a kiss, then give her sexy ass a firm swat. "We're going to be late."

"Best reason to be late ever."

I laugh. "I doubt Colt will feel the same way when he asks why our classes are unattended."

She lets out a little giggle. "We better go then."

The drive to the school is a quick one. I pull Mel in for a deep kiss before climbing out of the truck and circling around to her side. She smiles at me brightly as I help her down then tangle my fingers with hers to walk her into the building. She's radiating happiness, and I know it's because our relationship is back on track. I know that because I feel the same happiness pouring from my heart.

I'm so distracted by Mel that I don't notice Darlene until she practically pounces on Mel. She looks from me to Mel, then down to our linked hands and lets out a happy squeal. I shake my head with a smile at her antics. I'm glad she's happy for us. I know that Mel doesn't have many friends and Darlene is the perfect friend for her.

I drop a kiss to the top of Mel's head. "I'll see you later, kitten. Be a good girl."

She smiles up at me shyly and nods her head. Barely a second passes before Darlene is dragging her away from me. I watch as her ass twitches under her sexy skirt as she walks away. My cock already hard even though I just had her less than thirty minutes ago. I'll never get enough of her.

CHAPTER NINETEEN

Melinda

DARLENE GRABS my arm and tugs me away from Coop and into a big hug. She pulls away then leads me down the hallway towards our classrooms. The hallways are filled with students, but it's almost like we are in our own little bubble for how much attention they pay us.

"You look happy," she says slyly.

I smile up at her, practically beaming. "I honestly can't believe how happy I am. I've never been so happy."

"I take it you had a good weekend?"

I sigh. "The best weekend ever."

Darlene waggles her eyebrows at me. "So it's like that?"

"Yep," I agree, busting out in giggles.

Her face turns serious for a minute. "Everything is good with you guys?"

I let out a content sigh and lean against her shoulder as we walk arm in arm. "So good. He told me he loves me," I whisper-shout.

Darlene lets out a squeal that's loud enough to draw the attention of every eye in the hallway. "That's amazing! I'm so happy for you."

"Me too," I say, smiling happily.

The bell rings, interrupting our girl time.

"Dang it!" Darlene says. "Work calls. We'll chat later." She hugs me enthusiastically then runs off towards her classroom.

My morning classes go off without a hitch. The band is on point with our practice, and I think we are ready for our next competition which is a huge relief. I'm not sure why I'm always so paranoid about those kinds of things, but I am. Coop is right when he said we're an amazing band. My students are dedicated and willing to put in the work to be the best. Which is exactly what we are—the best.

My phone vibrates on my desk, and I smile knowing only one person would text during the school day. Sure enough, when I look, it's Coop.

I have to have lunch with a couple recruiters today.

My lips turn down in a pout. *I was looking forward to stealing a kiss, but work calls.*

Me too, babygirl. Are you behaving?

I send him a devil emoji. *Now why would I do that?*

To protect your sexy little ass from a spanking.

I laugh to myself. *Guess you'll just have to punish me, daddy.*

I can practically hear his low growl in response to my teasing. I shift on my seat, turning myself on just like I hope he's getting turned on. I've spent the whole morning hot and bothered after our quickie this morning. I'm wet and achy, completely ready for more. Not that that's a huge surprise, I'm always ready for more when it comes to Coop.

That can be arranged... He replies. *Love you, baby-girl. Behave.*

Love you, too, daddy.

I let out a happy sigh, something I've done a million times today. Since I can't see Coop for lunch, I decide to eat in my classroom and catch up on some grades. I finish up and grab my guitar. I start playing and lose myself to the music.

"Holy shit, girl," Darlene says from the doorway, scaring the crap out of me as the last notes of my song float through the air. "I didn't know you could sing like that."

I turn and smile wryly. "Apparently it's now the worst kept secret at Thurston Academy."

Weirdly enough, I don't feel uncomfortable or shy at being caught like I normally would. In fact, I feel good getting Darlene's praise. I'm changing... becoming more confident in myself and my talents, and I have Cooper's love to thank for it. I've become a stronger person with his guidance. Who knew that letting out my submissive side would create this new, stronger version of me?

"You're amazing, Mel. You could be a professional."

I shrug off that comment because regardless of her thoughts, I will never play in public. "Stage-fright kills any hope of that one dead."

"That sucks because you're so talented!"

"Thanks. I really just play for myself."

"So, Colt and I are going to The Playground on Wednesday, and I wanted to invite you and Coop. We can get dinner and hang out."

I smile widely at being invited. "Sounds like fun! I'll ask Coop."

She returns my smile. "Good! I've been itching to play," she says, and I have a feeling it's not the sexual kind of play. I'm sure she gets plenty of that from Colt. "Ugh, I guess I should go get set up for my next class. We are doing reproductions of Van Gogh this week... Nothing like a class full of Freshmen ruining the classics," she says, making her eyes go crossed and sticking out her tongue.

I laugh at her antics. "Better than hearing them butcher Mary Had a Little Lamb."

"Truth! At least it isn't my ears that bleed."

I roll my eyes and laugh. "Get out of here, trouble."

She sticks her tongue out but leaves. "Later!"

I LOOK IN THE MIRROR, frowning at my appearance. Coop comes up behind me and wraps his arms around my waist, meeting my eyes in the mirror. "You look beautiful, kitten."

I take in my appearance again. I'm wearing skinny jeans and a corset top that I once got for a Halloween costume but lost my nerve and never wore. I've never dressed like this before, but my goal has been to step out of my comfort zone... this is definitely out of my comfort zone. He's not wrong though... even I can admit that I look hot.

"Let's go before I change my mind."

He shakes his head, kissing my cheek. "If you aren't comfortable, change. You don't have anything to prove to anyone."

"It's just different," I say with a shrug.

"I don't want you dressing how you think other people want you to. I want you to be you."

I smile at him and cup his cheek. "And that's why I love you. But I think maybe... this is me? A different, more confident me."

He leans in and kisses my lips softly. "That's my girl. You ready?"

"Yep," I say cheerfully, getting excited for our dinner with Darlene and Colt. My first double date!

We ride in comfortable silence to the club, and, like always, he threads his fingers through mine as we walk side by side. My heart skips a beat at the sweetness. I love how he's always touching me. Even at school he finds little ways to touch me. Holding hands, a gentle touch to my lower back as we walk in the hallways, a sneaky kiss... he's always finding a way to show his affection, and I love it.

Darlene and Colt are already seated when we get inside. Darlene jumps up and hugs me. "I'm so glad you could make it!"

I smile happily. "Me too."

"We waited to order until you got here."

I chew on my bottom lip feeling slightly embarrassed because I know that I'm going to have a hard time picking my dinner. I always struggle. Every time I'm out with Coop he picks for me, and he's never picked wrong. I wonder if he will do it while we are with our friends or not.

I grab a menu and start perusing, trying to make my own decision. Once again, I'm tied up between the four-cheese mac and the chicken tenders and fries. Normally, when I'm with other people, I would order something a little more grown-up but being here at Teddy's, I can order from the "kid" menu, and it is acceptable. I do ennie meenie miney mo, but still can't decide what to order.

Cooper leans in and brushes my hair behind my shoulder. "What are your options, babygirl?" he asks lowly.

I look at him with a broad smile then show him

on the menu the two things I'm struggling to pick from. He kisses my neck below my ear. "I've got you, kitten."

I don't even try to hold back my happy sigh. My posture automatically relaxes, and I feel happy and free again. It's funny how letting Coop take charge of even this tiny thing makes me feel free. In this moment, he's my daddy, and I'm his babygirl and it's his job to take care of me.

I love it.

The waitress comes and asks for our orders. Cooper orders the chicken tenders and fries for me and a steak for himself with a side of the mac and cheese. Butterflies flutter in my stomach because I know he's ordered that so I can have a bite or two. He really is the perfect man. The perfect daddy, I correct myself.

Our food comes quickly, and just like I thought, Coop feeds me a couple bites of his mac and cheese, smiling at me when I happily eat from his fork. "Good?"

"Delicious, thank you."

"Anything for you, babygirl."

While we eat, the guys start talking about the football team and how they are on their way to the state championships. Darlene pulls a funny face, and we break off into our own conversation.

"Did I tell you that Charity accepted the job at Thurston?"

"No, that's exciting," I say, feeling less than excited that my best friend's best friend is obviously going to be moving here.

"Yeah, she's moving here over the summer!" she goes on excitedly, not noticing my distress.

Self-consciousness fills me up, and I start wondering where I will fall into her life when her true bestie is close. Darlene is the only friend I have, aside from Cooper... what will happen if she is too busy with Charity? What if I'm only her friend because her best friend lives a million miles away? What if she ditches me when Charity moves here?

Coop squeezes my thigh under the table and draws me out of my 'what if' downward spiral. Thankfully Darlene doesn't seem to notice that anything is amiss with me. I don't want her to catch on to my overly self-conscious thoughts.

"I can't wait for you to meet her. I know you'll become fast friends," she says excitedly.

Even though I have my inner doubts, I force them down and smile.

"She's coming to visit during winter break. We should definitely hang out... maybe show her around the club while she's here," she says with a conspiratorial wink.

I give her a surprised look. "Is she...?"

"Yep, kinky as fuck."

Colt looks at Darlene with a frown. "Watch that pretty little mouth of yours."

She looks at him repentant. "Sorry, daddy."

He snorts because despite her look and words, he knows she's anything but repentant. She's pushing his buttons on purpose. Not really being a brat, but definitely asking for a punishment in her own way.

Dinner is delicious and the company is even better. Once the guys pay the check, Darlene claps her hands excitedly. "Ready to play?"

My eyes widen and I wonder exactly what she has in mind. I don't want to offend her, but I'm definitely not into playing with dolls or anything like that. I'm honestly not really sure what kind of little Darlene is. It's never come up in conversation and feels like something too intimate to just outright ask a person.

"Yep, let's go!" I say excitedly despite my reservations.

She turns to Colt and bats her lashes at him. "Can we, daddy?"

He gives her an indulgent smile looking every bit the loving daddy dom. "Of course, baby. We're right behind you," he says. Both him and Coop stand to follow our lead to the club proper.

We make our way to the club, passing straight through the bar without pausing. Darlene pulls me straight to the giant playground in the middle of the room. Since it's a weeknight, it's not very crowded, which leaves plenty of space for us to have fun. On the inside, I feel like a giddy kid, brimming with excitement. I haven't felt so carefree in forever.

As a kid, it was always about shuttling me to the next music lesson, and there was very little time to just play and be a kid. Now, years later, I'm getting that chance, and it's all because of Cooper. I turn and give him a happy smile that he returns. He mouths the words 'I love you,' causing me to smile hugely at him.

Darlene finally lets go of my arm when we are standing in front of two empty swings.

"Do you like to swing?" she asks, seeming shy.

"It used to be my favorite thing. It's been forever though."

She smiles wide. "You're going to love this then!"

We both hop on our swings and start pumping our legs. The only thing missing is the wind in my hair, otherwise this feels like when I was a kid and I love it. Cooper and Colt are standing off to the side watching over us while they chat. Probably more sports talk. Boring.

Darlene and I swing until we are both breathless and laughing joyously.

"Hey girls!" Tessa says as she walks up beside us.

"Tessa!" Darlene squeals, jumping off her swing and running to the other woman and enveloping her in a hug. "Come swing with us!"

She chews on her bottom lip for a minute but

then nods her head. "I can do that for a little bit. I'm just on a quick break from bartending."

"Yay!" Darlene lets out another squeal showing how happy she is to be joined by our friend. She totally has embraced her little side, and I wonder if I will ever feel comfortable enough to do that. I guess swinging is a good start to connecting with that part of myself.

"Hey, Mel. How's it going?" Tessa asks.

"Good. How are you?"

She looks past me and over to where the guys are standing and makes a disgruntled face but doesn't answer.

Darlene leans in and whispers, "I see your best friend followed you over."

Tessa rolls her eyes and continues to watch the guys. I notice him right away. He's big... bigger than Cooper, which is saying something because Cooper is tall and built. He looks both scary and intimidating with his arms crossed over his chest. I think his name is Ransom, but I only met him briefly at Darlene's birthday dinner.

"Is he your boyfriend?" I ask innocently.

Tessa stops her swing and gives me a withering look. "Fuck no. He wishes he could control me."

Darlene's eyes widen, and she looks towards the guys, probably wondering if they heard what she said since she definitely didn't whisper. I realize that all three of the men are watching us. Ransom's jaw ticks, and he looks mad enough to spit nails. It's obvious that he heard her outburst. I feel terrible that I even asked. Especially when he looks so upset.

Cooper frowns at me, and I wonder if he's upset with me or if he's just frowning because of Tessa's words.

Darlene giggles and shushes Tessa. "You're gonna get us all in trouble!"

"I'd like to see that jerk try something," she mutters under her breath.

I give her a wide-eyed look then look back at Coop. He shakes his head and says something to an obviously frustrated Ransom, who then turns and walks away. No, not walk—he storms off with steam practically coming from his ears.

Tessa gets up from her swing abruptly and waves at us. "I'm going to get back to work."

"Sorry," I apologize. "I didn't realize..."

Darlene smiles. "Pssh, it's not your fault, girl. Tessa and Ransom have some kind of major history or something. Not that either of them are talking about it."

"I guess so..."

A few minutes pass by then Colt comes over and tugs Darlene against his chest with a growl. "You causing trouble, little girl?" he asks with heat in his eyes.

Darlene bats her lashes at him. "Probably," she

says. I instinctively know this is her way of asking for a different kind of playtime.

Colt gives her a devilish smile, then lifts her up over his shoulder like a sack of potatoes. She raises up enough to wave at me. "Thanks for playing with me. I had fun!"

"Me too," I giggle.

I turn my attention to a very scowly, completely over-the-top handsome Coop. "Were you causing trouble, too?"

I blink up at him innocently. "No, daddy. At least not on purpose. I was just curious..."

"Hmm... do you know what happened to the curious kitten?"

I chew on my bottom lip, not answering because I have a good idea what would happen to a curious kitten if Coop had anything to do with it. "No?"

"She gets her bottom spanked for causing trouble for her friends."

My eyes go wide and my core clenches at the threat. Part of me wants to jump up and run into his arms and beg for the spanking. It's been a long time since he's spanked me properly, and in a short time I've grown quite addicted to it. Another part of me doesn't want to be a bad girl. I want Coop to see me as his good girl.

"But I wasn't bad on purpose. I didn't know I would upset Tessa by asking her a question."

"I know, babygirl. You are my good girl," he says

lowly in my ear, causing shivers to trail up and down my spine. "That doesn't mean you're not going to get your bottom spanked."

Another shiver runs down my spine; my panties are getting wetter by the second at the threat of him spanking me. I wonder where he will do it. Will he take me to a private room or will we go home, making me anticipate the moment for longer?

Either way, I'm ready for it and all the good things that tend to come afterward.

"Let's go my curious kitten. Time for your punishment."

"Okay, daddy," I murmur meekly.

With a hand on my lower back, he leads me away from the playground and towards the private rooms. I smile widely, knowing I won't have to wait long to get what we both want. Instead of continuing to the private rooms, Coop leads me to the public punishment area instead. I swallow thickly, wondering if he's just trying to see how I'll react. I start to drag my feet, not knowing how I feel about possibly being punished where anyone can look and see.

"We don't have a private room reserved. I didn't plan on punishing this sexy ass tonight," he says, gripping my ass in his firm hold.

I let out a little whimper. "I don't know about this..."

"The best part about this arrangement is you

don't have to think about it. You just have to follow my lead."

I look up at him with caution. "I don't know if I can do this though..."

"I saw how turned on it made you to see the other littles punished here. The idea isn't appalling to you. What are your reservations?" he asks, his tone serious.

"I-I just I'm not sure I could actually go through with letting other people see me like that..."

"Do you trust me?"

"Of course I do," I answer without hesitation.

"Then trust me to take care of you. If it's too much, you tell me, and we stop."

I think about it. No, I'm not appalled by the thought of being spanked publicly. He's not wrong that it turned me on seeing the other woman with her red bottom on display. But could I be that girl? I don't really know, but I want to try. My wet pussy agrees with my naughty thoughts.

"Okay, daddy."

He smirks at me, his sexy dimples on show. "That's my good girl."

I practically swoon at being called a good girl. I love that more than I probably should. I live for hearing him call me his good girl. I could eat the words up and never be hungry for anything else ever again.

CHAPTER TWENTY

Cooper

MEL IS nervous about her spanking, but at the same time, I can sense her excitement. She's definitely not unwilling to get spanked publicly. Am I pushing her limits? Yes. Will that stop me? Fuck no.

I lead her over to a spanking bench and turn her toward me. I cup her cheek and look into her eyes, making sure she's still with me. There's another little getting spanked with a wicked-looking paddle a short distance away. Every thwack of the paddle makes my girl jump. Her attention keeps being drawn to the couple and away from me. I grip her chin and force her attention to me.

"Stay with me, babygirl."

She glances back to the paddle and looks back at me with genuine fear in her eyes. "I don't think I can do this..."

"What are you afraid of?"

Her eyes widen as if she can't believe I would ask that. "Paddles is a good start," she says.

I smirk raising my hands between us. "These are the only paddles touching your sexy ass tonight."

She visibly relaxes. "Oh."

I kiss the tip of her nose. "Yeah, oh."

"Ready?"

She nods, but I can still see her reservation.

I trail my fingers down her body, pausing to tease the tight buds of her nipples then lower to the button on her jeans. I hold her eyes as I slowly undo her jeans then push them down below her bottom, leaving her panties in place.

Without a word, I spin her around and push her over the bench so her ass is high in the air. I massage her cheeks, warming her up to the moment. I don't want her scared, just anticipatory. I pull my hand back and lay a couple light swats down. She wriggles and gasps, then relaxes down onto the bench letting out a long sigh.

I spank her over her panties a few times, getting her nice and ready for her punishment which is more like a funishment, but either works in this situation. She's not really in trouble. This is strictly for connecting in our power play. Me exacting my dominance over her and her letting herself sink into her submission—a reconnecting of our roles. We've reconnected our hearts and bodies; now it's time for us to reconnect as daddy and babygirl.

Now that she's in the right mindset for our scene, I tug her panties down, showing her slightly pink bottom. My cock hardens instantly. I lean over her and grind against her. "Fuck baby, this ass."

She groans and pushes back against me, teasing us both. I tsk her. "Naughty girl, teasing daddy like this."

"I can't help it," she whimpers. "I want you."

"Would you like me to pull out my cock and fuck you right here? Fuck you where everyone in the club can see you taking my big dick?" I growl. I know I'm saying the words, but I have no intention of doing anything of the sort. I'm too damn jealous to fuck her publicly like that. She's only for me. It's one thing to spank her, it's a whole other thing to put on a show of fucking my girl.

Mel doesn't answer me, she just moans lowly letting me know she probably wouldn't protest right now. She's turned on and not thinking straight. If she were in her right mind, she wouldn't consent to such a thing either. Which is why I'm simply teasing her with the prospect. It turns her on despite her not actually wanting it to happen, and that's my goal. Driving her crazy with lust.

I pull away and spank her with force. She gasps and squeals at the sharp sting drawing attention from onlookers away from the fierce paddling happening on the other side of the punishment area. I draw my hand back, spanking her again and again until her ass is a nice rosy red. I slick my fingers through her folds and groan at how wet my girl is. She moans, pushing her pussy into my touch.

"You're so wet, babygirl. You're enjoying your spanking way too much."

"S-sorry," she stutters. "I can't help it."

"I know, kitten."

I continue her spanking. My hand raising and falling in a harsh rhythm. She cries out and tries to buck up off the bench. I pin her lower back with my free arm, not letting her move. I spank her harder until she's whimpering. I stop spanking her and go back to teasing her pussy, dipping my fingers into the tight well of her pussy. Thrusting them in and out, loving the squelching sound it makes from how wet she is from her spanking.

"That's my good girl. Taking her punishment even though she didn't do anything to deserve it," I murmur in her ear, praising her like I know she craves as my fingers play with her.

I circle around her clit, teasing that little button before thrusting back inside her. "I'm going to come, daddy..." she warns.

"I know," I growl, redoubling my efforts to draw out her pleasure.

She shifts on the bench, trying to push back into my touch, but I've got her pinned so she can't move. "Please," she begs.

"Come for me then," I command, pinching her

clit.

With a low wail, she comes flooding my hand with her release.

"That's a good girl," I croon, stroking her through her orgasm until she's wrung out.

I put her panties back in place and pull up her jeans, leaving them undone, then pick her up and carry her to one of the many couches spread out in the area for aftercare. She snuggles into my hold, clinging to me like the little kitten she is, practically purring in pleasure.

I hold her in silence for long minutes as she comes back down to reality. She shifts in my lap and sucks in a breath at the pain in her bottom.

"Owwie," she complains, looking at me accusingly. "You hurt my bottom."

"It's not called a punishment because it feels good. Besides, you liked it," I say with a wink.

She scoffs. "I did no such thing."

"I'm pretty sure it's your pussy juices all over my hand."

She slaps my chest. "Don't be crude."

I laugh boisterously. "Just stating facts, babygirl."

She pouts, then cuddles back against my chest without another word. I run my fingers through her tangled hair and just enjoy the moment. Eventually, she rouses and looks around to see where we are. She relaxes back into my hold when she sees that no one is paying us any attention at all.

"How do you feel?" I ask.

"Sore... good... confused..."

"Why are you confused?"

"I feel like I shouldn't have liked that as much as I did."

"What part?" I ask.

"The whole public thing... it seems inherently wrong."

"There's nothing wrong with anything that we do together. If it brings you pleasure, then that's all that matters."

"I can't help wondering what other people will think of me if they knew I got turned on by being spanked in public," she admits quietly.

"No one here is going to judge you, and what happens in the Playground stays in the Playground," I say, trying to ease her worries.

"Like Vegas?"

I laugh. "Exactly."

"I think it'll just take some getting used to. Sometimes I feel like this whole situation is some kind of dream. If it is, I don't want to wake up," she says shyly.

I kiss the top of her head. "Me either, babygirl."

"I love you, Coop."

"And I you, Mel."

She lets out a happy sigh and lays back against me.

CHAPTER TWENTY-ONE

Melinda

"ARE you sure you don't want to sit with us?" Darlene asks for the dozenth time.

"No, I'm going to sit down by the team. Besides, you don't need a third wheel. Who knows if you and Colt might get a little freaky under that big blanket you brought."

She giggles. "This is true, though maybe a bit too inappropriate, seeing as we are at a high school football game."

I laugh. "Very true. Even so, I want to be close to Coop to cheer him on. It's not every day you play the state championships, and it be a rematch with their biggest rivals."

"If you insist."

"Come on, Darlene. Let's leave our favorite band teacher alone," Colt says, coming to my rescue and leading my best friend away.

"Later, guys!" I call out with a wave. I head down to where the team will be sitting and find a spot right in the center and settle in to wait for the game to start.

THE GAME IS TIED as the halftime show starts. Cooper and the team run off-field and to the locker rooms for what I'm sure is going to be one hell of a pep talk. I abandon my seat and follow after them, hoping to sneak a kiss when they head back to the field. I'm stopped on my way by Darlene and Colt.

"Oh my God, can you believe how close the game is?" Darlene shouts over the din of the crowd.

"I know. Our boys are on point, but so is the other team. It'll be close for us to pull it in for a win."

Colt shrugs. "We've got this in the bag."

I giggle. "Darn right, we do. Coop won't settle for anything but a win. Speaking of, I'm going to try to catch him before they get back onto the field."

Darlene gives me a quick hug then slaps my ass playfully as I walk away. "Go get 'em, girl."

I make my way through the crowd and draw up short from a familiar sight. That same woman is standing close to Coop, flirting. I narrow my eyes and straighten my spine.

Not this time bitch, I think to myself.

I'm not the wilting flower I was last time. I'm confident in myself and my relationship with Coop. She's not going to get between us again. I walk up to where they are standing and step between them. He looks down at me with a beaming smile while she turns her nose up at me.

"Who's your little friend?" she asks, looking down at me.

She's a heck of a lot taller than me, thinner, and all-around beauty queen pretty. I hate to admit that she makes me feel less than just by standing there in front of me, but I don't let that get to me like I once would have. Cooper is with me, not her. He obviously doesn't have a problem with my short stature and curvy body.

"This is my girlfriend, Melinda."

"Girlfriend," she scoffs. "Since when do you do girlfriends?"

I smile up at her, feeling a little petty at knowing she never made the cut for a potential girlfriend for Coop. "Since me, I guess," I answer snottily.

Coop pulls me into his arms and holds me close. "Just took the right woman."

"Whatever," she snarks and storms off.

I look up at him and shrug. "Wonder what her problem is."

He throws his head back and laughs. "She wasn't expecting my kitten to have claws."

I smile up at him. "Well, she was getting too

close to my favorite person. I'm territorial like any good kitty cat."

"Good. I only want you."

"Me too, daddy," I whisper just for his ears.

"I love you," he says, pulling me in for a passionate kiss. A kiss that has my toes curling in my shoes.

"Love you," I say breathlessly when he breaks the kiss.

"I gotta get back. Halftime is almost over."

I nod, still feeling dazed from his kisses. Somehow, I make it back to my seat despite floating on cloud nine and wait to watch my team kick ass. Which they do. They slaughter the other team. The second they call the game and announce the winners, Coop looks to me in the stands and marches right over to where I'm standing. He wiggles his finger towards me, indicating he wants me to come closer.

I don't hesitate. Of course I don't. Nothing could keep me away from my man when he's looking at me with fire in his eyes. He tugs me down from the stands and into his arms, kissing me in front of everyone like he wants to crawl inside me. Before, I would have felt embarrassment and hated every second of having everyone's eyes on me, but now I don't care. I like showing the world that Cooper Crane is mine.

I'm still reeling from his kiss when he drops

down on one knee in front of me. My hands go to my face, and I cover it in shock. Oh my God, is he about to...

"Melinda Young, you're everything I ever want in my life. Will you marry me?"

I gasp at the ring that he pulls out of his pocket. "Cooper!"

He smirks up at me, knowing that he's completely caught me off guard. I never in a million years guessed this was on his mind. We've only been dating a couple of months, but I can't see myself ever wanting another man. He's everything to me, and even though it's early, I want this. So bad.

"Yes! Yes, I'll marry you!" I scream over the roaring crowd, throwing myself into his arms.

Our lips meet in the middle, kissing each other. Showing the world how we feel about each other. I can hear the team whooping around us and celebrating not only their win but our engagement too. Then I'm gasping for a different reason when they pour cold water over the tops of our heads, highfiving.

Cooper and I pull apart laughing.

"I love you, daddy."

"Always, babygirl. Always."

EPILOGUE

Melinda

THE CLUB IS PACKED TONIGHT. Luckily Coop and I were able to snag a table at the bar for the evening. I look around nervously, waiting for Darlene and Colt to show up with Charity in tow. I met Charity last night at dinner, but I'm still trying to figure out my place in the dynamic between Darlene and her. Coop thinks I'm being silly at being worried about losing Darlene for a friend when obviously a person can have more than one close friend... I'm just feeling insecure, and I know it.

I can't help how I feel, though. I've never had friends like I do now, and it makes me anxious that things will be changing soon. Charity is just here to visit during winter break, get the lay of the land so to speak, but this summer she will be moving here and starting her new job at Thurston Academy as the cheer coach.

"Relax, kitten," Coop whispers in my ear, nuzzling my neck. "It's going to be fine; you'll see."

I take a deep, centering breath and release it, relaxing my shoulders and letting the tension flow out of my bones.

"Good girl."

I turn red at the compliment. I'm still not used to hearing it even after these last couple of months. I'm definitely not used to the reaction in my body at the words. My core tightens, and my panties dampen at his praise. I crave more of it. More of him. Always.

"Hey guys! Mind if I join you?" Tessa asks, sidling up to where we are sitting.

"The more, the merrier," I say.

She pulls out one of the empty stools and takes the seat beside me. "How's it going?" she asks, looking around the room. No doubt she's looking for Ransom. Probably trying to avoid the gruff, hulking man as per usual.

"Good. We're just waiting for Darlene and her friend Charity. Colt too."

"I forgot she was coming tonight. I'm excited to meet her!"

I smile at Tessa, wishing I could feel that level of excitement for my friend having her bestie here. I feel like an awful friend for the green-eyed jealousy I'm harboring. Because let's face it. That's exactly what this is. I'm fearful and jealous of sharing my best friend with someone she has a longer relationship with. I'm scared of being left out or left behind.

"You'll like her," I say, trying to feel genuine happiness.

Cooper grips my thigh and drops a kiss to my cheek. "I'm going to go talk to Jasper and Ransom. I'll be right over there." He nods towards the bar where I see the men standing.

"Okay, daddy. I'll be right here."

He growls, nibbling on my neck. "You better be."

I gasp and wriggle in my seat at the tease. He knows exactly what attention to that particular spot does to me. In case you can't guess, it drives me insane with lust. My pussy is wet, and my clit throbs, wanting attention that I know it's not going to get until much later.

"Tease," I chastise without any heat behind it.

"You know it, babygirl." He pinches my bottom before sauntering away.

Tessa lets out a little sigh, looking longingly at the ring on my hand. "You guys are so perfect together," she says wistfully.

"Are you okay?" I ask, sensing the change in her mood.

"Yeah, just a little melancholy these last few days. Nothing a bit of fun won't cure," she says, brightening up to her usual peppy self.

I've noticed the last few times we've been here that her and Ransom seem to be at each other's throats more and more. They are like gasoline poured on a flame when they are together. I get the feeling that it's not hate that she feels for him, but I could be wrong.

Before I can dwell on it, I see Darlene and Colt pushing through the crowd along with a wide-eyed Charity as she takes in everything the club has to offer.

"Hey girls!" Darlene says with a flourish before hugging both Tessa and me. "Sorry, we are late. The princess couldn't decide on what to wear," she says, pointing her thumb back at Charity.

I giggle a little because I know exactly how she feels. I still have a hard time picking out my outfits, but I'm getting better at feeling at home in my own skin. No longer confining myself to baggy, shapeless clothes. As Darlene has pointed out, I radiate a confidence I've never felt before. I have Coop to thank for that. He's really helped me come out of my shell and prove to myself that the world isn't some big scary place. I even took part in a karaoke contest here at the club—I totally won too.

"Charity, this is Tessa," Darlene introduces. "And of course you met Mel already."

Tessa stands from her seat and, ignoring Charity's outstretched hand, hugs her in that exuberant way she has about her. "Nice to meet you. Welcome to The Playground."

"This place is crazy," Charity says, sounding a little bit in awe of her surroundings. "I've never been to a club that caters to people like us before. This is like a little's paradise."

We all laugh at that because it's true.

"I'm going to go chat with the guys. Will you be okay here with your friends?" Colt asks Darlene.

"We will be fine. Shoofly, go have a nice chat with your manly friends, leave us girls to our girly talk."

Colt growls and spanks her ass for her cheek. "Watch yourself or I'll have you over my knee and paddled before you get to hang out with your friends."

She smiles at him. "Promises promises."

He shakes his head and wanders off to where the guys are hanging out.

"So, do you want a tour?" Darlene asks Charity.

"Absolutely, but first, I want to know about tall, dark, and handsome over there talking to Colt," she says, fanning herself. "He's hot."

Tessa glares at Charity but then turns and sees that Colt is talking to Jasper, and Ransom is nowhere to be seen. Her face turns pink, and I swear she relaxes, realizing that it's not Ransom she's talking about. Interesting. Maybe there is more to their relationship than I previously thought.

Darlene titters. "That's Jasper."

"Is he single?" she asks. "I'd hate to lust over someone else's man, but damn he's hot."

We all giggle at that. "He's very single," I say.

She stares at the guy longer than is polite, her attraction clear on her face.

"Want me to introduce you?" Darlene asks.

"No way. He's eye candy and nothing more. Besides, I'm only here for another three days. You know I'm not looking for a temporary fling."

Darlene nods. "Then how about a tour of the club instead?"

"Absolutely. Show me all that The Playground has to offer."

We give her a thorough tour of the club. She ooh's and ahh's at everything. "This place is perfect," she finally says when we are back in the bar. "I can't wait to move here and become a member."

"I feel like I should say, 'I told you so,'" Darlene says, pursing her lips.

"Yeah, yeah, yeah. Yuck it up. You were right. This place is great."

"It's nothing like the clubs back home," Darlene says. "It's a whole different world here."

We sit and chat for hours, talking about nothing

and everything. I relax the more I'm around Charity and Darlene. I don't feel in the least bit excluded like I thought I would. It feels like we've always been friends, and I love it.

COOPER

"Jasper," I say for the third time, trying to get my friend's attention.

"What?" he barks, drawing his eyes away from where the girls are sitting a few feet away. He's been staring ever since Darlene came in with her friend Charity.

"Jesus, man. What crawled up your ass and died?"

He scrubs a hand down his face, shaking his head. "Nothing, just tired. Been working long hours on this job. Who knew private security was more exhausting than being a police officer would be? Not to mention it's a thankless fucking job when you're working for rich pricks."

We all chuckle at that because Ransom tried to tell him, but the stubborn ass wouldn't listen. Even though he's complaining, I know he loves his new job. He was burnt out on being a cop and working within the confines of the law. Private security is less... structured.

Jasper's eyes wander back towards the girl's table. "Tell me about Darlene's little friend," he asks Colt. "She looks familiar, but I can't quite place why."

"That's Charity. Her and Darlene have been friends for years, and she's the new cheer coach at Thurston. She'll also be coaching girls' physical education. If you listen to Darlene tell it, she's the best of the best in everything she does."

"Is she single?" he asks, shocking the hell out of me. Jasper never asks about women and their relationship status. He finds his play partners in the club and doesn't do attachments.

"As far as I know, yes, she's single. She moves here in a couple months. She's just here for winter break right now."

He nods like what I've just said is the most interesting thing he's heard all night, never once taking his eyes off the woman.

I slap him on the shoulder, grabbing his attention once more. "Well, guys, I think it's time I swooped in and swept my fiancée off her feet. Talk to you later."

I prowl towards Mel, giving her a hungry look. She looks up at me as if she can feel my eyes on her. She nibbles on her bottom lip and returns my hungry stare. It's always this way with us. We are starved for each other every second of the day.

"Sorry, ladies, but I'm going to steal my girl," I

apologize half-heartedly a second before I pull Mel off her seat and throw her over my shoulder. She lets out a little squeal of surprise but doesn't protest. She simply tells her friends bye making promises to see them for brunch tomorrow.

"Where are we going, daddy?" she asks, wrapping her arms around my waist from behind.

"Private room," I growl, thinking about all the things I have planned for her.

"Okay." Is her only response, but I can tell she's excited by the way she wriggles her body over my shoulder.

We get to the private room, and I toss her on the big bed, crawling on top of her, so she's pinned beneath me. Before she has a chance to catch her breath, my lips are on hers. I brush my tongue over her closed lips, and she instantly opens for me like I knew she would. My tongue glides between those sweetly parted lips, and I kiss her hungrily. Our tongues dance together, sliding along one another, dueling for control.

Mel lets out a little whimper when my hand lightly encircles her throat in a reminder of who is in charge here. Despite being reminded of her place, she still kisses me feverishly, and I can hardly punish her for that. My cock is thick and hard behind my zipper, begging to be let free. She rocks against me and I just know her panties are soaked with her sweet honey.

I release her lips and kiss down to the front of her corset top. My girl has gotten more and more confident since we started dating. She no longer feels the need to hide behind her clothes, not that I care what she wears. She would be gorgeous in a burlap sack but knowing that she's confident and happy makes me happier than I've ever been in my life.

I make quick work of untying her top. As soon as her breasts are free, I take one turgid peak into my mouth, sucking on the berry-sweet nipple.

"Oh, Coop," she moans my name, and I growl into her soft flesh. I nip her sensitive tip, and she gasps at the slight pain I inflicted. "More," she begs.

Who am I to deny my sweet kitten anything? I lavish her breasts with attention as I work her skirt down her legs until it's discarded on the floor along with her top. It's then I notice that Mel isn't wearing any panties under that sexy skirt of hers.

"Naughty girl," I snarl. "You mean to tell me you've been bare under your skirt all night?"

She nods. "Yes, daddy. I thought it would be a nice surprise for later."

I growl. "Anyone could have looked up that short skirt and seen what's mine."

Her eyes grow wide as she realizes that she's in trouble. "I-I didn't think about anyone else being able to see... only you, daddy."

My tone softens because I know she did it for

me and only me. "If I had known you were bare for me, I would have dragged you off sooner."

"Next time, I'll tell you." She barely breathes out the words in a whisper-soft voice. She's just as turned on as I am by being naked under her skirt for me.

"There won't be a next time unless we are safe at home where no one else could potentially see what's mine."

"Okay, daddy," she readily agrees.

I stand from the bed and tug her with me until she's standing before me in all her naked glory. I admire the swell of her breasts and the curve of her hips. She's fucking perfection. I don't know what I did to get so lucky, but I'll never take it for granted.

Sitting on the end of the bed, I pull her belly down over my knees. She wriggles excitedly. My girl has grown to love her spankings, especially when they are over my lap. She's told me that she likes the intimacy of it so I make sure to spank her like this often and well. Especially when she doesn't deserve it.

I quickly lay down three swats to her cheeks, loving how the jiggle from the impact of my heavy-handed palm. I squeeze her bottom, rubbing in the sting. It doesn't take long for me to work up a rhythm that has Mel writhing on my lap, trying to wriggle away. She loves her spankings but also loves fighting against how much she enjoys them.

I spank her until her ass is a bright pink and warm to the touch. As this isn't a punishment, I stop long before tears can fall. No, tonight I want my girl moaning my name. I need her crying out for her daddy in mindless pleasure.

Her folds are wet and glistening when I slide my fingers through them. She moans as I tease over her clit then pump my fingers deep inside the hot well of her cunt.

"Oh, God. Daddy," she moans.

"You enjoyed that spanking a little too much," I accuse.

She whimpers as I tease up her crack and circle her puckered ring. We've been working up to anal sex, using my fingers and plugs to get her used to the stretch of taking my cock. Tonight is the night she's been begging for. Tonight, I'm taking her sweet pussy, then I'm going to fuck her tight ass.

"I can't help it, daddy. It hurts so good."

I slowly tease my finger against her ass, lightly pushing. Not enough to enter her, just enough to drive her crazy. She's been begging for this moment. At first, she was scandalized when I told her I wanted to fuck her ass, to own every part of her, but when I started playing with her, she became excited by the prospect. Now when I play with her ass like this, it hardly takes a tease to her clit before she's coming like mad.

I lift her off my lap and stand her on shaking

legs. I stand in front of her, tilting her head back with a knuckle under her chin. Her lust-filled eyes meet mine, and she lifts on her tiptoes to kiss me. Her hands fist in my shirt. She opens her lips for my seeking tongue. I lose myself in her kiss, letting her lead for the moment before I wrench all control away.

"I love you, daddy," she moans into my lips.

"Mmm, babygirl. I love you. Now, up on the bed. Hands and knees," I correct when she starts to turn to lay back.

She climbs up, settling in on her hands and knees. She looks back at me with desire in her eyes. I strip off my clothes quickly, then kneel behind her. I spread her cheeks, admiring her wet heat. Her little clit is peeking out of her folds, begging for my mouth. Not one to disappoint, I lean in and lick that swollen bundle of nerves.

Mel gasps and pushes back into my mouth. I slap her ass in reprimand. I control this moment, not her. She whimpers but ceases her movements. She knows I will stop if she doesn't and that's the last thing she wants right now. I flatten my tongue and lick her from clit to asshole. I twirl my tongue around that tight ring of muscle causing her to jerk at the sensation.

I keep teasing her ass while I slip two thick fingers deep into her cunt. I thrust them in and out, hitting her g-spot with every motion. She whimpers and whines as I build her pleasure up and up until I can tell she's ready to come. I stop before throwing her over the edge, not letting her find her release.

"Please," she whines.

"Not until I say, babygirl."

I move back to her clit, sucking the tender nub between my lips and nibbling on it lightly. "Oh..." she squeals. "Daddy. Please!"

I decide to have mercy on her. "Come," I command. I redouble my attention on her clit, fucking her deep with my fingers. She explodes on my mouth, and I lick it up, eating every drop until she's shaking in my hold. Her upper body collapses to the bed, pushing her ass further in the air.

Before she can recover, I kneel behind her, lining my cock up with her pussy and slamming into her. She screams my name as I fuck her hard and fast. My balls draw up, and it takes every ounce of my self-control not to come inside her right here and now. Her pussy clamps down on me as she comes for a second time tonight.

I massage her bottom, coaxing her through it. She whimpers when I pull out then gasps in pleasure when she feels the head of my cock press against her bottom hole. She moves forward, away from my pressing cock.

"Relax, babygirl," I coo. "You can take me."

I stroke her ass and back until she's relaxed and ready for me. This time when I press against her, she pushes back helping me enter her.

"Oh God, you're huge," she gasps.

Not wanting to scare her, I don't tell her that she's barely taken the head of me. I reach down and slowly pet her clit. She instantly relaxes into the touch, taking another inch of my cock. Not wanting to hurt her, I snap open the lube I set aside when I undressed and drizzle the cold liquid on my dick. I slide in the rest of the way with very little resistance. Mel cries out when I'm fully inside and clenches down on me.

"Shh... it's okay. Just breathe. You'll get used to me."

"N-no," she whimpers. I'm one hundred percent ready to pull out and stop at her stuttered word, but her next words are music to my ears. "Felt good. Too good..." She moves forward then pushes back against me with a guttural moan. "Move, daddy."

Normally I might reprimand her for being bossy, but I can hardly fault her for telling me to do the very thing I want to do most in the world. I pull out until just my head is poised inside her, then slowly enter her again. I fuck her like that for several strokes making sure to be careful. The last thing I want to do is hurt my girl.

"More..." she says. She tries to force the issue by

pushing against me, but I grip her hips hard, stopping her.

"I don't want to hurt you."

"You won't. Feels so good... so fucking good."

I smirk at her dirty words. My girl doesn't curse often, and I love the loss of self-control. She's telling me exactly what she wants without an ounce of shyness. Far be it for me to deny her.

I pull out and slam back into her.

"Yessss," she hisses.

I repeat the motion over and over until I set a punishing pace. She loves every second of it, just like I knew she would.

"Fuck, babygirl. You're so goddamned tight like this. I'm not going to last long."

"Me either," she gasps.

"Are you going to come with my big cock in your ass?" I growl.

"Yes! Oh, God. So naughty..."

"That's right. You're a naughty girl coming for daddy's fat cock buried deep in this tight ass."

She clenches down around me and screams out her release. Dirty talk gets her every time. She loves my filthy mouth.

"Fuck, fuck, fuck," I grunt, fucking her harder. Flicking my hips forward and back in rough drives that have my balls drawing up tight. I pull out of her ass and pump my cock, releasing my seed over her ass and pussy.

She moans when I rub my release into her with my fingers. I circle her clit and push my fingers deep into her cunt. Her muscles flutter around me as her orgasm ebbs away. Mel collapses to the bed and I lay beside her, tugging her against my chest.

I push her sweaty hair off of her face and kiss her slow and sweet.

"You okay?" I ask.

She lets out a pleased sound and nods.

"Words, babygirl."

"I'm perfect. Boneless. Maybe a little braindead."

I smirk down at her. "Good. That means I did something right."

"Mmm," she murmurs.

I lay with her for a moment longer then get up to clean us up. Once that task is taken care of, I crawl back into the bed with her. She cuddles up against me and promptly falls asleep.

I kiss the top of her head, happier in this moment than I've ever been. Mel is everything I could've asked for and more. She's the love of my life, and I can't wait to spend forever with her.

THE END

Want more from Mel and Coop? Check out their

bonus story or find it here: https://
BookHip.com/ZRMPQRH

Did you miss Darlene and Colt? Read their story
here.

ALSO BY RORY REYNOLDS

CONTEMPORARY ROMANCE

DARK CONTEMPORARY ROMANCE

Unforgettable

PARANORMAL ROMANCE

Dragon's Thief

Dragon's Curse

Dragon's Hope

Dragon's Ruin

Dragon's Treasure

Dragon's Fire

ABOUT THE AUTHOR

Rory Reynolds is a stay-at-home mom of two little monsters. She's a ravenous reader of romance and firmly believes that you can never have too many book boyfriends.

She writes feisty heroines, alpha heroes, and panty drenching smut with happily ever afters.

SUBSCRIBE to my newsletter and get a free book.
http://roryreynoldsromance.com

BB bookbub.com/profile/rory-reynolds
f facebook.com/AuthorRoryReynolds
O instagram.com/RoryReynoldsBooks

Printed in Great Britain
by Amazon

16207686R00140